Destiny Finds Her

By

Miranda Lynn

ACKNOWLEDGEMENTS

This book wouldn't have made it this far if it weren't for a great many people. I want to take a moment to thank them all. First off, my husband Ryan, without whose support I wouldn't have continued on once I got the words out during my first NaNoWriMo. Secondly to my writers group who are always excited to hear the progress I have made. To my writer friend, critique partner, and historian extraordinaire Terry. Thank you for all your Facebook chats and for always pushing me outside of the box. To my editor Jennifer, you took my rocky manuscript and refined it to what it is today. My cover models Frederick Schmitz and Charis Sims, my photographer Kat Bradshaw, and my cover artist Robin, with very little direction from me you created an amazing cover that I just love to sit and stare at. I can't wait to work on the rest of the series with you all.

I want to thank Deena Remiel and Amber Scott for talking to me years ago and being honest about the independent author route. Along with all my other author friends, there are too many to list here, but I hope you know who you are.

And most of all I want to thank my friends, family, and fans. Thank you for purchasing my first book, I hope you enjoy it as much as I enjoyed writing it. Book two is already in the works, so if you love Jami and her story, share it, shout it, review it, and wait with baited breath for the next one.

CHAPTER 1

Brock gazed into her eyes, reading her intentions, and was overwhelmed by what he saw there. He couldn't escape those eyes. He pulled her toward him, wrapping that supple body into his arms. She fit his body to perfection. They seemed to melt into one. As he lowered his head to take her mouth, all he could think about was devouring that perfect pout and bringing out the passion he knew hid underneath her shell of propriety.

His tongue snaked out to trace the outline of her lips, while his hands roamed over her rear. He wanted to touch her skin, gradually. He could never get enough. She had slithered her way into his heart. He needed to fill her to completion, now.

I lost focus as an insistent vibrating started to annoy me.

What the hell? I was just getting to the good part. Of course, I forgot to shut my phone off. I forgot I'd put it on vibrate during my doctor's appointment. I sat and stared out the window of what I called my study. Really, it was just a small alcove I'd shoved my favorite reading chair and a couple of rickety bookshelves into. My little haven. In my mind it was a library, complete with a roaring fireplace and walls upon walls of bookshelves, lined with more books than I could read in a lifetime. And this was my perfect window seat. I didn't see the dirty, dingy building out my window, but rather hills of heather and wildflowers with a haze rising off them in the early morning light.

I picked my book up, but couldn't focus. I was restless. A walk might help. The one crowning glory to my apartment was the great walking trails out behind the building. You wouldn't know it from the front, but all the properties along this road butted up to a great wooded area someone had been smart enough to put walking trails through. I opted to take the stairs today instead of the elevator. Since I only lived on the third floor, it was a nice warm up to the walk.

When I hit the outdoors, the overwhelming stench of car exhaust and garbage overtook me. I quickly walked around the building and headed into the woods. About twenty steps later, the air cleared and I smelled the fresh scent of damp earth, pine needles, fallen leaves, and wildflowers. I never understood how the stench of the city didn't permeate here, but I didn't dwell on it much. This was my oasis, my haven from reality in a way. I increased the volume on my music and stared walking.

I took the same path each time, but halfway through I noticed another path, one that hadn't been there before. I was still really restless, and if I kept on my normal route, I'd feel unsettled when I returned. I decided to explore a bit and took the new path. It went further into the trees than I'd been before. The canopy overhead got thicker, which made it darker along the path. I muted my music to listen to the sounds of the woods. The chirping of the birds seemed happy, and I thought I heard water running.

"There is no water in these woods," I said, just to hear someone speak. I followed the sound, but the closer I got, the less I heard around me. The woods had gone silent. I rounded a corner, and in front of me was a little creek. Not really a creek though, more of a babbling brook. I glanced around, expecting to find a little leprechaun or a tiny fairy. It seemed too good to be true, something my imagination created, not something in the middle of town.

This place was magical, out of place, unreal. Streams of sunlight broke through the canopy of trees resting on a perfect little outcropping of rocks. I couldn't resist the temptation and went to sit down. I closed my eyes and raised my face to the sunlight, sensing energy around me. I couldn't explain it, but for the first time in a very long time, I was at peace. This place calmed me and settled my nerves better than a pumpkin spice latte ever could.

I must have fallen asleep, because when I opened my eyes, the sunlight was gone and shadows had fallen around me. I stood, the water continued to flow, and I promised myself to visit again. I headed up the path toward my apartment. I had a book to finish. Time to find out what Brock and Aggy had in store for them. After months of reading, I'd finally found a manuscript that moved me and was worth sending on to the senior editors.

The sense of calm I awoke with at the brook stayed with me throughout the evening. The manuscript had sucked me in. After finishing the novel, I stretched and realized how late it'd gotten. Wondering what time it was, I grabbed my now-empty coffee mug and headed to the kitchen, stretching the kinks out of my body as I went. The stove clock read two a.m. I blinked twice to make sure I'd read it correctly.

Suddenly, time caught up with me. I decided against the refill and made my way to the bedroom. I noticed I'd left my reading light on at my alcove. Knowing it'd bother me, I went to turn it off.

As I reached my chair, I saw my laptop still on. I needed to send a quick email before hitting the hay. I sat to type it up quickly. I hit send then checked any new mail I might have gotten and noted an advertisement from my best friend Todd's travel agency. Occasionally, he sent me emails with the newest travel packages. "Scotland." I couldn't resist opening it. That destination was a dream of mine.

Maybe if this manuscript panned out and the publishers took it, I would be able to take a short vacation. Knowing I could probably never afford it, I opened the email to find the first picture to be an exact copy of the brook I'd found on my walk earlier. A sense of déjà vu overtook me. I sat up, a bit startled. It couldn't be. I'm sure there were many creeks and brooks that looked alike in the world, but I'd swear the rocks in the picture were exactly the same as those I'd laid upon today.

My eyes must just be playing tricks on me. After reading for so long, they were tired. I was just seeing things I wanted to see. As I scrolled through the information and what the package cost was, I caught a faint whiff of heather on the breeze from my window. I was definitely tired.

The bottom of the email simply said, "Call Me."

That's odd. Todd always put the prices in the emails for me. He knew I had a dream board, and with a price to set a goal for, I could always keep myself motivated. Heck, that's how I was able to take that cruise to the Bahamas two years ago. I made a note to call him in the morning, then closed down the laptop, shut my reading light off, and went to bed.

CHAPTER 2

I woke the next morning, a bit groggy and in need of my morning coffee. I walked out to the kitchen, realizing I hadn't set up the pot to brew this morning. I'd have to wait for it to perk. That wasn't like me. No matter how late I stay up, I always set the coffee to perk before I wake up the next morning. Sighing to myself, I cleaned out last night's cold sludge and set a fresh pot to brew.

After deciding a hot shower would help wake me up, I detoured back to the bedroom, grabbed my standard yoga pants and tunic, and headed into the bathroom. Catching a glimpse of myself in the mirror, I grimaced. There is a reason I don't look in mirrors before my first cup. My hair was a mass of rat tails the color of chocolate, highlighted with natural deep red. As I ran a wide-tooth comb quickly through it, I looked the rest of my face over. Not bad, round with just a smattering of freckles on my nose that no amount of makeup would help. My eyes tilted a little at the corners, and my eyelashes were the envy of my best friend Todd. He pays good money for the fake ones to get the same effect.

Stepping back, I perused the rest of my body. Boobs, slightly larger than I would like for my five-foot-nine frame, and already a bit droopy. Curves everywhere they should be and no wayward pooches. Satisfied, I hopped in the shower.

Once I'd toweled my hair off from the shower, I went to check my email. The first one was from the publishing house with a revised edition of the manuscript I'd just finished reading. I forwarded the email to my boss, telling her this one was a keeper in my opinion. I gave her my feedback and reasons why, and sent the email on.

I smelled the coffee wafting in from the kitchen, so I closed out my email, pulled up the screen saver, and went to get my first cup.

That cup was a sacred thing to me. I savored it every morning; my big mug, wrapped in my hands as I let the aroma entice my eyelids to open and my senses to fully awaken. I added my sugar and creamer before curling up in my chair to take that first sip.

The flavors swirled around and found each taste bud before trailing down my throat and wakening each organ on its journey to my awaiting belly. The warmth curled there before venturing out to each extremity. By the time I got to the bottom of my first cup, I was ready to start the day. I checked my notepad to see what I had in store for the day. The only thing jotted down was to give Todd a call about the email he'd sent me last night.

Todd has been my best friend since college. He was the first person not after me because of my family name, money, or what I could do for him. He is funny, flamboyant, and dresses me better than I dress myself most days. He is also smart, talented, and can sell an around-the-world cruise to a fish. At just over six feet tall, he has surfer-dude hair, a year-round tan (thanks to self-tanner), blue eyes you can get lost in, and a smile that lights the room. He is the perfect guy, aside from the fact that he bats for the other team. Always my luck. But he has been there to get me through many a rough important dinner, as well as dances with my mother. You should have seen the first time she met Todd. Only he could find an electric-blue Armani suit and pair it with powder pink!

Todd didn't get into the office till ten, normally. That could wait a bit. I went to get another cup and realized the time. Eight a.m. I had two hours before I could call him. Plenty of time for a walk, and I was impatient to get to the little brook. Mornings were always more magical in the woods, and it'd be the perfect time to explore the area a bit more.

I opted to leave my mp3 player at home this time, wanting to enjoy the sounds of nature instead. I headed around the apartment and to the area toward the trees. I couldn't remember exactly where I found the new path, so I took my time walking, enjoying the atmosphere around me. It didn't take long to find it again.

After turning onto the path and picking up my speed, I was at the little brook before I knew it. The water seemed to be flowing stronger today, but I could still see straight to the bottom. It wasn't a very deep stream. The stones on the bottom were pretty; little rounded pebbles in varying shades of gray, brown, blue, and green. Further up, a few larger stones sat in the middle of the brook, creating an obstacle for the water to flow around, producing little bubbles and that soft musical sound I think of when I hear the words "babbling brook".

I took a seat on the stones and pulled my knees up to my chest, resting my chin and just taking it all in. Moss crept up the stones on the bank, giving way to a lush carpet of grass and wildflowers. Again, I smelled heather, but couldn't pinpoint where it was coming from. Heather couldn't survive in this climate, even next to this little brook. It must be the combination of all the wildflowers' scents mixed together.

My eyelids became heavy. This seemed odd as I'd rested well last night and hadn't been up that long. I sat there, feeling a bit hazy and sleepy, and noticed a small creature venturing up, maybe to drink from the brook? It wasn't a squirrel. The tail wasn't long enough. Maybe a chipmunk, though the markings on the fur weren't right. This wasn't anything I'd seen before.

I watched it, trying to decide what animal family it could be from, when it looked up at me. It stared right into my eyes. I gawked, my eyes widening when I realized this little creature's eyes weren't the little black dots I would expect, but a misty gray seeming to swirl as if a fog was contained within them. This little creature winked, and then scampered away.

I shook my head. My imagination was running away with itself again. I attempted to move, but my body had other plans. Instead of finding myself standing, I'd actually lain down. My eyes got heavier the longer I rested. *A small nap can't hurt.* I had no pressing work, and the call to Todd could wait. I closed my eyes and let the sun warm my face as I drifted off to sleep.

"Jami," a voice whispered.

Startled, I sat up and shaded my eyes.

"Jami, dear."

I scanned the trees, trying to locate the owner of the voice.

"Down here, dearie."

Peeking down, I found that the little creature who had scampered away was in fact at my feet, gazing at me. I drew my feet up quickly.

"I'm dreaming." I scanned the area again. "Who's there? This isn't funny."

"Yes, dear, ye are dreaming and please quit thinking of me as a creature. I have a name, and it's Roma."

I stared at this little creature with its round black eyes and fluffy, multi-hued brown fur. I rubbed my eyes. Sure enough, she was still there. "But, how?"

"It's a dream, dearie. Anything can happen in dreams"

"Who or what are you?"

"As I said, my name is Roma, and all ye need to know is I am here to help ye. To give ye a bit of advice"

"What kind of advice?" Heck, if this was a dream, I may as well play along. It could make for a great story if I remembered it when I woke up.

"Keep an open mind and an open heart. Yer fate is going to show itself to ye soon." Roma skittered away into the trees.

"Wait, what the hell is that supposed to mean?"

Roma stopped. "I have said all I can. I am not to interfere, simply to guide. That is all I can tell ye right now." She disappeared into the foliage beneath the trees.

"Wait, Roma, come back!" I jumped up and followed her, but when I got to the trees, she was gone. *Damn small animals. I need to wake up and go home.* I went to sit down on the rocks. *Okay, if I close my eyes again, when I reopen them I'll be awake.* Seemed logical to me. We're supposed to be able to control what happens in our dreams. I tried to relax, closed my eyes, and waited. Once I'd counted to sixty, I opened them, feeling no different and pretty sure I was still dreaming.

Am I awake now?

No, my dear, yer quest in this dream is not done, a different voice responded inside my head. I wasn't tired anymore, and knew I wouldn't be able to force myself awake. *I guess I'll explore a bit.* If this was a dream, I wondered what my subconscious had in store for me.

I followed the path to where my apartment building should be. The walk took much longer than I remembered. The grass got thicker the farther I went, instead of thinning out as it should. The trees finally gave way to a field of wildflowers and the path continued through it, but there was no apartment building in sight. In fact, the city was gone. I followed the path up a small hill until it crested. My breath caught at what I saw.

Sprawling before me was what I could only describe as a castle. The first one I'd ever seen in person. A huge stone wall encircled the small cluster of huts and the large main building. The huts were made of wood, mud, and thatched roofs. At the crest, near the wall, stood an impressive stone structure, which I imagined was the main house. Herds of sheep grazed in the fields outside the walls, and I heard cattle bellowing somewhere off in the distance. A paddock of horses was enclosed inside the wall as well. There were other structures, but I couldn't tell what they were from this distance.

This is what I'd always envisioned a Scottish keep to be. All I had to do to get there was follow the path down the hill and through a small field of heather. Instead, I chose to sit and watch for a while. Afraid of what I might find if I followed that path, I was content to sit and watch the kids running around just outside of the wall, playing some type of game. An older boy watched over the herd of sheep as plumes of smoke curled out of the chimneys of each of the huts. A tingling sensation ran through my veins as I watched this live fantasy before me.

Everything seemed so surreal. I swayed in the sunlight, and was so focused on the children in the valley, I didn't hear someone walk up behind me.

"Who are ye?" a male voice asked.

I shrieked and spun around. A wall of trees greeted me. I was beside the brook, next to the stones I'd fallen asleep on. I took a moment, and a few deep breaths, to calm my beating heart.

Wow, what a dream. I dusted myself off and headed toward my apartment. I needed to write this dream down while I could still remember it.

This will make one hell of a story.

CHAPTER 3

17th Century Scotland

Devlin O'Rourke had to get out of there. Between Donovan and his politics, Darrick and his nightly carousing, and Mama and her iron-fisted family ruling, he couldn't take anymore. Volunteering to walk the patrol seemed a good idea at the time, anything to get out of that room.

The kids ran and played as Devlin walked through the courtyard on his way outside the gates. He could've ridden the perimeter, but he needed more time than that, so walking was the better option. They weren't really in any danger of gangs of bandits attacking during the daylight, so Devlin was confident in his choice.

On his way through the gates, he saw the children running, and the young O'Malley sitting on a stump playing a lively jig for them. It was always a joy to see the children enjoying themselves. It was coming up on the Harvest Festival, and soon the courtyard, as well as the surrounding fields, would be filled with neighbors, friends, traveling troupes, and wanderers. All coming to celebrate the changing of the seasons and the great bountiful harvest they'd been blessed with this year.

Walking down the well-worn path along the tree line surrounding their land, the atmosphere calmed his nerves. The soft bleating of the sheep and the intoxicating smell of heather and wildflowers that gave way to the tangy scents of damp earth, decaying leaves, and fresh pine needles were relaxing. It was these things that brought Devlin to himself. The land grounded him and made him feel calm and at peace.

Always on alert, his senses attuned to every breeze or rustle out of place, he continued on. The sound of the children and the fiddler echoing down in the valley just barely reached his ears, providing a pleasant background melody. He sighed as the sun peeked out from behind a cloud to shine down upon the children. This was his land, his pride and joy. His heart swelled at all he saw.

As he ventured further along the tree line, the birds started chattering and became restless. The squirrels quickly climbed trees, hiding in their little holes. Devlin's ears strained to hear what they were hearing. He stepped into the tree line, and faded into the shadows, awaiting what threat might come. His hand went to the hilt of his sword, muscles tensed, ready for a fight. What he saw next was completely unexpected.

A young woman treaded softly out of the trees, along one of the many paths the healers used to forage for herbs and fetch water from the brook, a woman Devlin had never seen. She was not garbed in the traditional broadcloth dress, but in pants and some type of jerkin. He'd never seen such clothing. Her hair was pulled away from her face and high atop her head, in a small circle with a tail flowing to her shoulders. Much like a horse's tail. He stood silently, waiting to see what she'd do.

This woman was not from around here; that much was obvious. His muscles coiled, ready to pounce should she take off toward the keep. She simply sat down on the top of the hill, in the rays of the sun, and watched the children. She seemed to be in awe of what she saw in front of her.

Devlin wove silently through the trees to the path she'd emerged on. Advancing with years of learned stealth, he moved up behind her. When he was within a few steps, she still was unaware of his presence.

The breeze brought a whiff of her scent to him. A sweeter smell Devlin had never encountered. His body reacted immediately. His knees went weak as he breathed her in.

"Who are ye?" Devlin demanded, sounding a bit gruffer than planned.

She jumped, and was gone. Like a ghost into the night. He couldn't believe his eyes. Glancing down, he saw the slight indention from her footsteps. He followed them down the path until they abruptly ended at the brook. He searched the area for her campsite or any signs of where she'd come from. She was a mystery.

After minutes of searching, a sound wafted up to his ears. Tilting his head, he recognized the bells of the gypsy troupe that travelled through the lands. It was time for him to head to the keep and resume the duties of middle son.

The cart pulled to a stop only feet in front of him.

"Good day, Devlin O'Rourke, second son of Margaret and Donovan O'Rourke. I hope we find ye in good spirits this glorious day."

"Good day to ye, Alexandru. I hope yer travels have gone well." Devlin gave a slight bow of his head to the elderly gypsy.

"Yes, young one. Travels have been well this year, though me old bones may not always agree. I am getting to be a bit too old and weary for the constant travel. This may be me last year, so we must enjoy it as best we can."

"Oh, Father, ye have many years to come. Let us go set up camp," a feminine voice stated from the shadows of the cart. "Thank ye, Mr. O'Rourke, for welcoming us onto yer land. We would be honored if ye would join us at our campfire tonight."

Alexandria, the eldest daughter, emerged from the cart with a smile. She'd grown over the past year. Her hair was raven black and traveled down her spine unfettered. The bells sewn into the hem of her skirt chimed as she moved to sit on the driver's seat, waiting to help her father into the cart. The rest of her body had filled out quite nicely as well. She'd be turning many heads at this year's festival.

His eyes roamed over her, taking in her womanly curves. Their gazes met and she gasped. He peered into eyes that seemed to be older and wiser than her years.

Alexandria nodded to her father. "It has begun. He has seen her."

"Hush child," her father whispered, as he ushered her across the seat. "Please disregard the girl. She knows not what she speaks of. I would be honored to have ye at our camp tonight." Taking the reins, he prepared to maneuver the cart out into the fields.

"I would be honored to share yer camp." Devlin inclined his head in farewell before he guided his team off the path. "Until tonight."

Entering the gate, Devlin bellowed for Christan, knowing he'd be close, awaiting his return.

"No need to bellow, old man. Here I am."

"Ah, Chris, ye need to take over the border patrol for me," he informed him.

"Again? But ye just came from there. Did Alexandria fluster you so much it slipped yer mind?" Christan chuckled.

"Och, ye arse, I didn't finish. I need ye to go out to the path I just came from and finish the round. With guests arriving, Mother will want me close at her side."

"Ah, well in that case, I will see ye at evening meal." Christan pulled aside one of the young boys and instructed that his horse be readied. "Are we expecting any skirmishes?"

"No, just make sure all is well before the festivities start tomorrow. I don't see the Mulligans trying anything so soon after the beating they got last time."

"Aye, Brother." Christan chortled. "Twas a rather fun day, wasn't it?" He slapped Devlin's shoulder.

"Aye, it was. Till evening meal." Devlin left Christan to his duties.

Horse hooves beat a rhythm behind him as he made his way to the keep, ensuring Christan was on his way. His mood became foul as he entered the kitchens. His mother's voice was echoing through the great room, reminding him of her promise to finish their earlier talk.

With the marriage of his older brother a year past now and the new babe on the way, his mother had her sights on him. At twenty-eight, he was in no hurry to tie himself down with a wife and bairns. His freedom was precious.

"Bring the bathing tub and hot water pails to me chambers," Devlin bellowed, and escaped up the servant's stairs to his chambers.

After disrobing and encasing himself in the hot water, Devlin leaned his head against the tub, closed his eyes, and drifted off. Dreams of the mystery woman filled his head, and his body with a throbbing. Reaching down to ease his desire, he vowed to learn her identity before the festival was over.

CHAPTER 4

Current Day

A knock sounded at my door just as I'd dialed Todd's number. Checking the peephole, I was surprised to see a deliveryman standing there. I signed for the package and mouthed a "Thank you," as Todd's charismatic voice floated over the phone. I love to tease him because he sounds just like Jack from "Will and Grace".

"Hello, Travel Treasures, how may I help you?"

"Morning, Jack, err, Todd. Aren't you chipper?"

"Karen, err, Jami?" Todd took a deep dramatic sigh. "You know that joke is getting kinda old: need to rework your material. How's life with you?"

"Going pretty good, though I've received a summons from Mother."

Todd laughed. "Oh, girl. What is it now?"

I sat down in my chair and opened the envelope. "An official request for my presence at the annual Christmas Ball." I gagged.

"Oh, glitz and glamour. How are you going to pull that one off, Miss Sweats and Yoga Pants?"

"Hey, I can clean up when I want to. I just don't normally want to. I like being comfortable."

"So, when are we going shopping for the dress? When is it, and do you need a date?"

"Hang on. Let me read through the invitation and I'll let you know the details, and of course you are going. I can't deal with an evening around my mother without you."

I opened what resembled an oversized Christmas-ball ornament with a ribbon at the top, and set it on the table, trying to figure out how to get the invitation out. The ribbon was actually holding it closed. Pulling the ribbon allowed the sides of the ornament to open and reveal a scroll inside.

"Wow, if she donated half the money she spent on these invitations to the charity, she wouldn't need to have the ball in the first place." Sarcasm dripped from my voice.

"Yes, but then, dear, how would she get all those celebrities and snobby upper-crust people to fawn all over her? You know she lives for that Hamptons spotlight."

"I know. I never did fit in with that crowd," I sadly admitted.

"You didn't, darling. You are so much better than that. There isn't a fake thing about you. So what does it say? When do we get to go and do some primo people watching?"

"We have three weeks to prepare. The ball is on October seventeenth, at seven p.m., at the Hampton House. She's opening it up especially for this event. I haven't known Mother to hit the Hamptons in the fall. Ever."

"Wonder who she's trying to impress?"

"I don't know, but that's not why I was calling. I got your email last night about the Scotland trip, but you didn't put a price on it. I need to know what times are available and such."

"I didn't send you an email. And how did you know about Scotland? I just got the details about it myself this morning. I had made a note to send it to you as soon as the flier is ready."

"I think you had one too many last night, because I'm looking at it right now. The picture is what hooked me, the one with the babbling brook in it."

"Whoa, wait a minute. Let me scan through the pictures I have for it. Hmm, there's not a single picture of a brook. Jami, what's going on?"

"I don't know. I just know what I have in front of me. I'll forward it to you, and you send me the Scotland info you have. Maybe this was just an automated email. You do those occasionally, right?"

"Well, yeah. I don't remember setting it up for you, but hey, it's been busy lately, maybe Lacey set it up and forgot to tell me. That girl is a bit flighty, but she knows her marketing stuff. How about I come over after I close up shop and we can hunt up a dress for you? I can bring the Scotland info then."

"Sounds good. I'll see you then."

"Bye, doll."

I hung up and pondered how the email had gotten to me. Shrugging, I decided to start searching for a dress. I abhor shopping, doing most of it online, though I will admit to a weakness for shoes. I don't have many pairs, but that is the one thing I could go out shopping for, spending hours drooling over all the shoes I wish I could have. Shopping with Todd was even more fun. At least he gives me an honest opinion of what flatters my figure and what makes me resemble a fool. He's the reason I have the one pair of Minolo's in my closet. They're so lonely that I take them out and wear them around the house so they don't feel completely useless. I haven't splurged since I bought them. Maybe it was time to again.

Todd showed up just as I'd made a fresh pot of coffee that evening. He came in with his arms loaded with dress bags, shoe boxes, and even dainty lingerie bags.

"What the hell?" My eyes bugged out.

"I figured it'd be easier to bring the store to you, since it'd be like pulling teeth to get you out on the town." Todd grinned mischievously.

"Oh, for heaven's sake, how did you do it? I know all your credit cards combined couldn't have paid for one pair of these shoes, let alone everything else."

"I just had to throw your mother's name around a bit and the salesgirls fell at my feet to help. Everything is on loan, and whatever you pick will go on your mother's account."

"You know I don't want her money. It's why I haven't touched the trust. Dammit, Todd, now she'll have something to hold over me."

"No, she won't. If she wants you there so bad, she won't blink an eye at paying for the clothing. Trust me; it'll be fine." "She called you, didn't she?"

"Yup, right after I got off the phone with you. She must have had the delivery guy call as soon you got the invitation. I was supposed to be hush-hush about it, but hell, woman, she even offered to pay for my tux. Armani at that."

"You are such a clothes whore. All right, set everything up in the bedroom. You want some coffee?"

"Coffee? Are you crazy? I brought a bottle of Dom along with all these wonderful clothes, on your mother's tab as well. We're doing this in style."

I shook my head, laughing, as he waddled his way to my room, laden with all those packages. I glimpsed the shoeboxes again and my mouth started to salivate. I grabbed two champagne glasses, washed them quickly, and followed Todd.

"All right, darling, go undress, put on your robe, and let me get things set up," Todd instructed.

"Undressed, really? When did you switch sides?" I winked at him as I headed to the master bath.

"You vixen. It'll be easier to get you to try them on if I already have you unclothed."

"Fine," I said through the door. "You win this time."

"Darling, I always win."

I laughed so hard I almost cried. I was down to undies, as I was sure Todd had picked up a few backless dresses, and in my terry robe, I went out. Todd had set up a viewing area with the two wing-backed chairs I had in my bedroom, and one small vanity table between them holding the champagne and glasses.

"Sit down, darling, and let me pour you a glass." He quickly uncorked the bottle and filled my glass.

"Oh boy, starting with a full glass. This should be good." My nerves kicked into gear. Todd could sometimes be a little over the top when he dressed me up. I remembered the ensemble he tried to get me to wear to my first gallery event. I shuddered at the memory.

"I know what you're thinking, and I have matured. My style is much better than the fiasco of 2007," Todd said with a sniff.

Across from me, on nails where my pictures usually hung, were six garment bags with shoe boxes lined up beneath them. I was more interested in the shoes, but I sat and allowed Todd to reveal them one at a time. We had Prada, Valentino, Armani, something couture— Versace, I thought—Stella McCartney, and Dior. I couldn't wait to see what shoes he'd paired with each dress.

"I tried to keep them all in style or design to go with your jewels. Your mother suggested I stop by Tiffany's and pick something out to go with these, but I knew it'd be useless. You always wear those emeralds of yours."

"I know my mother can't stand them because of what they mean. They point out her one flaw, the fact she could never bear children herself." My gaze dropped to my hands.

"So, doll, what are we trying on first?" Todd asked with forced cheer in his voice.

"Well, why don't we just go down the line?" I took a large swallow of champagne and stood to unzip the first dress.

A simple, elegant, black sheath with a low back, V-neck front, and a slit up one leg to mid-thigh.

I dropped my robe and slipped it on over my head, then peeked over my shoulder. "Zip me up, darling"

Todd did as I asked and turned me around. "Very elegant, the lines are great, but kind of boring," Todd assessed.

"Well then, let's add the shoes." My eyes rounded at the prospect of seeing what he'd picked out. "OMG! How did you get your hands on a pair of these?"

In my hands was a black pair of Louboutin Eugenie stilettos.

"Magic, darling, and let's leave it at that. With this dress, the shoes had to make the outfit."

I tried them on and fell in love. But he was right; the dress was a bit boring.

"Doesn't feel right; let's move on. Though I think I'm going to cry as I take the shoes off." I sat and slowly slipped them off, then lovingly placed them on their pillow.

"You could always keep the shoes just because. You deserve at least that for what your mom has put you through," Todd teased.

"And where would I wear them? No, they get returned. I don't want any more ties to her than needed."

The next dress didn't feel right, either. Stella McCartney never really fit my style. I quickly moved on. I didn't even glance at the shoes that went with it. After trying on the fifth dress, I sighed at Todd. "I sure hope this next one is better. I don't feel like going out to shop and, after this, I'm not sure I can handle another at-home spree, either."

I unzipped the last garment bag and gasped. This was it; this one spoke to me and I could hear the hum coming from the emeralds in my drawer.

"Versace Couture," Todd whispered. "You'll love the shoes, too."

I leaned down to open the shoebox and squealed. Jimmy Choo's, his Kiln design.

I hugged Todd. "I could kiss you for these"

"Hurry up and try the dress on, too. Don't get me wrong, the shoes are sexy as hell by themselves, but you can't go to this shindig in just the shoes."

Todd helped me out of the robe and dropped the dress over my head. It molded to my body as it slid down. It was strapless, and the top was a corset flowing into a long, slightly-flared skirt. The material flirted with my shape, and I had a sudden rush of warmth course through me, causing my skin to take on a healthy glow. *What the hell? How can I be getting excited by a dress?* It was just a dress, but so much more. As Todd finished with the laces, I heard my jewels humming loudly.

"Get the emeralds." I stepped into the shoes as he brought the velvet case over. I sensed a slight vibration as I put them on. They were happy, I could tell. Don't ask me how. I just could.

I went over to the full-length mirror and didn't recognize the woman staring at me. The dress was a midnight black, with a sheen of emerald green that appeared as I moved. The color flowed along the dress as I swayed and pivoted. It hugged every curve and shimmered around me. The skirt whispered as I twirled around to watch it swirl.

"Perfect," Todd and I said in unison.

"Return the others. This is it." I turned to find him gone. I glanced around the bedroom, then heard the bathroom door shut. I walked over to the champagne bucket and poured another glass.

The more I walked around the room, the more the dress caressed my skin. I was getting impatient, waiting on whatever he was doing in that bathroom. Another tour around, then out to the living room, and through the kitchen to turn the coffee pot back on. Upon returning to the bedroom, I glanced at the bathroom door. Todd stood there in his tux. He sauntered up next to me and we both stared into the mirror.

"We are gonna knock their socks off. The image we make together is stunning. You won't have any choice but to have fun, Jami."

"I suppose not. As long as I am on your arm, we can do anything. Too damn bad you bat for the other team. We're so perfect together."

"Honey, if I didn't bat for the other team, as you put it, you wouldn't be dressed this damn good. You think a straight guy could have put that ensemble together?" He laughed and went to change out of his tux, stopping to fidget with the laces at my back. "Now, I loosened the laces for you. Carefully take the dress off so we can put it up till the party. Wouldn't want to ruin it now, would we?"

Todd and I sat and chattered the evening away, finishing off the bottle of Dom he'd brought.

"Well, I think it's time for the fairy godfather to pack up his things and flitter off. I have a full day ahead of me tomorrow, and I need my beauty rest." Todd stood and packed the rest of the clothing and shoes up. "Oh, here, almost forgot to give you the Scotland info." He grabbed an envelope from his messenger bag.

"Thanks, just what I needed to finish out my day. I can gaze at these and daydream myself into sleep." I chuckled.

"Well, really think about this one. That is the best price I've ever seen for Scotland, and you can take up to a year to travel. Just let me know if you want me to book it."

I saw Todd to the door. "You know I will. Have a good night and be safe."

Todd kissed my forehead. "Sweet dreams to you, little Jami."

I took the Scotland folder to the bedroom with me and snuggled under the covers, paging through the information. Todd was right; the price was unbeatable and the options were out of this world. Basically, I could plan where, when, and how I wanted to go. I put the information aside and picked up the pictures of all the places to choose from. I got to a pile of eight-by-ten pictures. They were breathtaking ... and then I saw it.

My brook.

The one I'd walked to the last two days. It was exactly the same all the way down to the cropping of rocks I sat on. One difference, though. In the picture, a book sat next to the rocks. The cover was leather with some sort of symbol burned into it. No picture, no title, just a leather-bound tome.

That clinched it.

Tomorrow I'd call Todd and tell him to book it.

I put everything in the folder, set it on my nightstand, and clicked off the lamp. Curling up, I pictured the valley of heather I'd dreamed about earlier that day. I wanted to see it again.

CHAPTER 5

17th Century Scotland

I sat on the hill again. There was something new in the valley. An encampment of sorts. Music and bells echoed up to me. The grass next to me rustled. I jumped and found Roma staring at me with those stormy eyes.

"Keep an open mind and open heart, Jami." She bounded into the heather and scuttled toward the camp.

My body became heavy as the sun began to set. I couldn't keep my eyelids open. I lay down in the heather and let my eyes fall shut. Utter blackness closed in around me quickly, and I floated.

Beep, beep, beep, beep!

My hand swung out to hit the snooze button. I dragged myself into a sitting position and slammed the alarm off for good. While rubbing my eyes, I sniffed, and the intoxicating aroma of coffee hit my nostrils. My mouth watered and I stumbled to the kitchen.

I poured myself a mug and started whisking the cobwebs from my brain to plan my day. *Call Todd. Email Mother about the ball. Take a walk to the brook. Write down that dream from yesterday.* But first, snuggle up in the chair and enjoy the first of many mugs of coffee.

After about half an hour it was time to get motivated. I dropped off my empty mug in the kitchen, threw on my tennis shoes, and headed out the door. Time to visit the brook again. I was drawn to that spot. Feeling a bit restless, I picked up my pace and made it there in half the normal time. While surveying the area, the breeze carried the scent of heather to me again. I sat on the stones, leaning over to trail my fingers through the water. Out of the corner of my eye, I saw something resting against the far side of the stones. I reached over to find a book that resembled the one I saw in the picture last night.

With shaking hands, I laid it upon my lap. I just stared at it, dragging my fingers over the Celtic design engraved on the cover, trying to make sense of it. It couldn't be the same book. I had to get to the apartment to compare it, but I couldn't move. I sat there waiting, and like before, my eyes got heavy. My body felt weighted down and I couldn't help but lie on the shore. I curled around the book, my fingers still tracing the cover as I drifted off to sleep.

"Jami, come. Ye must hurry."

I recognized Roma's voice immediately. I searched the ground for her little furry body.

"Stop searching. Ye must hurry. Meet me at the tree's edge."

I walked down the same path I took last time I dreamt of her. At the tree's edge, I saw the large keep and its surrounding lands, with the same encampment outside the walls. There was a small covered wagon with a fire built not far from it. Two mules were tied up, happily grazing on the heather. I searched for Roma, but was unable to find her, so I ventured to the hilltop where I'd sat before, only a few steps out of the trees. Deciding to sit and wait, I gazed down at the keep and, in all the hustle and bustle going on, I noticed a young woman walking up the path toward me. I tried to find a hiding place quickly, but there was nowhere to go except for the tree line behind me. Knowing that if I moved, she'd most certainly see me, I stayed put.

I watched her as she made her way up the path toward me. She raised a hand in greeting. There was nothing aggressive or menacing in her gesture, so I waited for her. My instincts told me she wouldn't do me any harm. I raised my hand slightly to return her greeting, with my heart racing, and the blood rushing through my veins. The breeze picked up and swayed the heather as she approached.

"Jami, I'm glad ye stayed," she said as she reached the crest of the hill.

"Who are you, and how do you know my name?"

Her eyes met mine and suddenly I knew. I'd seen those eyes before. With a sharp intake of breath I asked, "Roma?"

"Yes, Jami." She inclined her head "May I sit with ye?"

I nodded, still staring at her eyes, trying to work it all out in my head. "Who are you? What are you? Where am I, and what do you want from me?"

"I cannot answer all yer questions, Jami. Those are for ye to find out in yer own time." She lowered her eyes. "Just know I am here for ye, to help guide ye to yer destiny. I cannot tell ye more than that."

"Can you at least tell me where I am?"

"Where do you think ye are?"

"I think we are in Scotland, but I don't know of any keeps still functioning. And the way you dress ... is this some type of reenactment, and why do I only see you and this place when I sleep by the brook?"

"So many questions. Aye, ye are in Scotland, and aye, that is a fully-functional keep. But no, we are not a reenactment. This is our life."

"Alexandria," someone called in the distance.

"I must go. I cannot spend too much time in yer presence. Just know I am directing things here and we await yer arrival. Trust in yer instincts, hold the book close, and be open to all possibilities. Ye will find the truth in time." Roma stood and skipped down the hill, the bells on her skirt tinkling as she went.

Hoof beats sounded and I quickly hid in the trees.

I wasn't quite quick enough.

"Stop right there," the rider yelled. He urged his horse to a trot to catch up with me, as I took off running toward the brook. If I could just get to the book, all would be fine. I'd wake up and the dream would be just that. A dream.

It sounded like the rider hopped off his steed and followed down the path after me. I ran as fast as I could, but he was faster, and caught up with me as I reached the water's edge. He grabbed me, and I started to thrash around, trying to break free.

"Wake up, wake up! Dammit, Jami, wake up!" I chanted over and over, my eyes squeezed shut.

"Och, stop thrashing around, woman. If ye still yerself, I will not hurt ye," my pursuer said in a voice that brooked no contest.

I stilled myself, trying to calm my breathing and keeping my eyes closed, waiting to wake up.

"All right, that's better. Now tell me who ye are and where ye come from," he said into my ear.

A shiver went down my spine. "My name is Jami and I am not from here." I clenched my fists, trying to still the shaking that began to take over my body. "Will you please let me go? I just want to go home."

"And where might home be, little one?"

"New York."

"Oh, so ye are British, are ye? Well, now I don't think I can let ye go. The laird will want to know about any foreigners sneaking around our woods."

"I'm not British. I'm from New York. You know, in the United States."

"United States? I know no lands by that name. I believe this is a matter for the laird to decide upon."

"If you just let me go, I can get home. I won't bother you. I just want to go home," I whined in defeat, knowing I might not make it home if I didn't reach the brook.

"Please just let me sit down a minute, I'll try to explain everything. I swear. I'm not armed, check for yourself, but please just let me sit down. I don't think my legs will hold me much longer." If I could just get to the brook, I could make it home.

He let go of me with one arm, but left the other still tightly wrapped around me. He quickly searched me, satisfying him that indeed I wasn't armed. "Aye, ye are telling the truth. I find no weapons. What is a woman doing in these woods with no type of weapon? Are ye trying to get killed?" He slowly walked me over to the brook. "I will let ye sit, but know I am faster and stronger than ye and, should ye try to escape, I will think nothing of hunting ye down again."

I nodded. My legs crumpled and I was glad the brook wasn't far. I collapsed on the bank and put my head in my hands. I breathed deeply to calm myself and glanced up into the face of a warrior. He had chiseled features darkened by hours in the sun, a body hardened by battle, and eyes that spoke of a kindness the rest of his body didn't. "Thank you. What's your name?"

He seemed to be fighting with himself. His eyes took on a strange glaze. "Christan."

"Well, Christan, I have no idea where I am, or even when I am, because I don't think I am in the same time anymore. I can't explain it to you. There's no way of explaining right now. I think I may be losing my mind."

Christan seemed to be taken aback. He wavered from foot to foot, then took a step closer. With his movement, a stream of sunlight hit me. I had to squint up to see him, then he was gone ... or maybe I was. My eyelids fluttered closed. *Not again.*

I woke up shaking my head, cradling the book to my chest. When I glanced around and verified that I was back home, I headed to my apartment. This was getting weird. My brain was going into overload trying to figure it all out. I tried to shut it down and search for that gut feeling I could always count on.

I didn't find what I expected. Instead of scared, run-for-your-life vibrations, my instincts were calm and peaceful. My body had warmth to it, and the symbol on the book in my hands glowed.

I thought it was time to visit my past again. Something was going on and I needed to find out what. With my twenty-fifth birthday approaching, things were starting to change. I needed to know why.

CHAPTER 6

Current Day

I went straight to my bedroom, opened the top drawer in my dresser, and pulled out the box my birth parents had left me. I sat on the bed and ran my hand over the engraved top. My heart raced, and I was a bit scared to open it. Every time I did, my body reacted to it. Things were happening I couldn't explain, and I'd been ignoring them for years, but I couldn't ignore it any longer.

I sat there, afraid to open the box, remembering the day I got it. I remember like it was yesterday. The moment I was told the truth; when I knew I would never live with my mother again. I went to a hotel, checked in, and took the box with me. It was there that I opened it for the first time. It contained an envelope, a folded letter, a picture, and a jewel case.

The aged picture depicted a field of heather with a castle in the background. The same castle as in my dreams. Just looking at it gave me a sense of calm. I smelled the heather and was drawn to that place. I made a mental note to figure out exactly where it was. I set it aside with the jewels and chose the folded letter. It was written on thick paper stock, aged over time.

Sitting on the bed in the hotel room, I closed my eyes, took a deep breath, and very carefully unfolded the letter.

Dear Jami,

I don't know how to start. I know you must have a lot of questions, and I only wish I were there to answer them in person. First, you should know your mother and I love you with all our hearts, and giving you up was the hardest decision we've ever had to make. Our hearts will bleed a little every day from this day on. If we could change things and keep you with us, we would, but for your safety, we can't. We are being hunted. You are being hunted, and we have to hide you in the only place we thought safe: another's family. I can give you some information and I only hope it's enough for now. We ask that you wait to open the envelope you will find within this box until your twenty-fifth birthday.

You were born in Scotland. I can't tell you exactly where, because if you are anything like me, you will take off straight away to learn all you can. You have much to learn before you're ready for that adventure. Your name is Jami, short for Jamison. I know, not a very feminine name, but one that has deep meaning in our family. That was one thing we made sure of when we made the arrangement with your adoptive mother. Jamison is a very strong name and carries with it a power that will unfold as you grow older.

I know none of this makes much sense. You come from a very long line of powerful women. Each generation has a unique power, but they also inherit a bit of their mother's and ancestor's power, making each generation stronger than the one before. I don't know what your powers will be, but I do know we have done all we can to help you unleash and harness them.

We will be reunited in the future, that much I know is true, though when and how I am unsure. Just know the little voice inside you and your instincts are trustworthy. Trust in yourself, be open to the possibilities, and always—always—follow your heart. Don't let your head get in the way of your true self and your true happiness.

You may be confused, and most likely hurt and upset with your mother and I, but it was for your protection. I want you now to take this box and the things inside and find yourself. The jewels will help guide you; they are yours. They sang to you the day you were born and will sing to you till the day you pass on. They will help you, guide you, and always come to you. Keep them hidden in a safe place, and wear them when you need protection and clarity. They will unlock your true self when you are ready.

Jami, we love you and know if you listen inside yourself, you will

find who you are and find us.
  I love you eternally,
  Dad

That was it, the most confusing letter I'd ever read. No name saying who he was or who my mother was ... and Jamison. Yeah, I've hated that my whole life. People figured my parents were closet lushes because of it. Seriously, naming your daughter after a bottle of whiskey, though no one ever said anything to my adoptive parents. They were too powerful for that. Money bought power these days, and the Morgans had plenty of that. So, I, Jamison Morgan, was teased in private, but never in public.

I stared at the envelope. I could open it now and find out everything, but something inside told me to leave it. I folded the letter from my father and put both it and the envelope in the box. I propped the picture up in the open lid and grabbed the jewel case. Feeling a pull from the pit of my stomach, I opened it. My fingers found their way to the intricate weaving of metal between the stones. It wasn't pure gold or silver, but a mixture. Amazing. Awe-inspiring." As my fingers wandered over the cuff bracelet, it heated in my hand. And when I touched the stone in the center, it hummed. I put it on and my whole body tingled, like my insides had turned to liquid. Suddenly, I was exhausted. I placed the picture under my pillow, then pulled the bed covers down and climbed in, with the cuff still on and humming me to sleep.

I noticed the design on the cover of the book was the same as that woven into the jewels. This book was somehow a piece of my history; it was a piece of me, my family. I needed to find out what that design was.

When I awoke, I was a bit scared to open the book. My instincts told me to wait, so I did. Instead, I put things away in my box, except for my cuff, and put the box in its hiding place. It was time to wear the cuff again. The nice thing about it was I could wear it on my wrist or my upper arm. I could have it on without others knowing. Today I wore it beneath my sleeve. Having that warmth there was a comfort. I stored the book beneath my pillow. I'd revisit it later.

I headed out and opened my email, opting for a nice mug of tea this time, instead of coffee. There weren't too many emails, a couple that were junk, and a message from Todd.

Jami,

Keep the datebook open all day for the Christmas Ball. Already booked us a full day of pampering and preparation. See you Saturday.

-T

Crap, it'd completely slipped my mind that the ball was coming up. My mother is a bit odd. She has a Christmas Ball, but holds it almost two full months before Christmas, so she can make sure everyone comes. That way, it won't interfere with family and friends who want to get together the month of December. I never believed her because we never got together with anyone in December. I think she just wanted her December calendar open to attend all the other functions with the rich and famous.

It also escaped my notice this year that the ball landed on my birthday. I don't know what she'd planned, but I was certain I wouldn't like it. I intended to stay only as long as necessary, then Todd and I would hightail it out of there.

I opened my calendar to mark the day. If I didn't, I'd forget, and letting Todd down was unacceptable. He was so looking forward to going. At least I could enjoy it through him.

The other email I opened was from the publishing house; another book to read and evaluate. I downloaded it to my e-reader and shut down the laptop. I needed an afternoon escape from reality, and hopefully the new manuscript would provide just that. I refreshed my tea, grabbed my afghan, and snuggled in for a long afternoon of reading.

CHAPTER 7

17th Century Scotland

Christan searched around him, rubbed his eyes, and searched again. It didn't help. The woman was still gone, like a puff of smoke. There one minute and faded into the air the next.

"I have been too long without a woman. My mind is now conjuring them out of thin air."

He made his way to his steed, finding him exactly where he'd dismounted, happily munching on some heather. Christan had trained him extensively; you couldn't find a better warhorse. He grabbed the reins and launched up into the saddle.

"Let's go home, ole boy." He nudged his steed toward the path through the heather, opting to take the shortcut to the keep. "A nice flagon of mead and full meal should help rid me of these visions. Tomorrow we will head out for a nice run to get rid of both our pent-up energies. What say ye, boy?"

The horse snorted and shook his head in agreement.

Christan dismounted and handed the reins to the groom greeting him at the gates.

"Give him a good rubdown, and see he is stabled with fresh hay and oats."

"Yes, sire, right away," the boy answered, and led Christan's steed off.

Christan made his way up to the keep amid the hustle and bustle of the people, smiling and nodding greetings to the clansmen as he went. Upon reaching the peace of the laird's house, he headed straight for the great room, finding a comfortable chair by one of the two large fireplaces flanking the room. He positioned himself to be out of the way, but still able to observe everything around him, with his back to the wall as his training had ingrained. A warrior never left himself vulnerable, even when relaxed.

He waved one of the housemaids over. "Bring me a tankard of mead and a plate of meats and cheese to fill my belly."

She bowed and took off to fulfill his wishes.

While Christan waited, he observed the frenzied pace the workers had about them, getting the great house ready for the festival. They expected many guests, and this would probably be the last time he'd have to relax before returning to his duties.

An overflowing plate and tankard were placed in front of him. "Is there anything else I can get ye, sire?" the maid asked, staring at his boots. The females of the house were taught to keep their eyes down, so as not to invite any unwanted advances from males.

Donovan had made that clear when he became laird. The staff in the keep were not available for anything more than their normally appointed duties. He did not stand men trying to take liberties with the females of his clan. He protected them all as if they were his own blood. And if there was an interest in one, the man had to go through him first and properly court them. If they were just in the mood for a quick tumble, there was a whorehouse in the next village they could visit.

"No, thank ye," he replied. "That will be all."

She curtsied and returned to her duties.

Christan sat observing her as he ate his fill. Though his senses were alert to the goings on around him, his mind wandered a bit and he wondered about the woman he'd found. Was she really just a figment of his imagination, or was there something else going on? Her clothes and demeanor intrigued him. He'd never seen a woman around here dressed as she, and her accent was unknown to him. He barely understood what she'd said.

The fire warmed him. The winds had been a bit chilly out on the hills. They carried the first signs of winter. It wouldn't be much longer before the first flakes of snow fell. The Festival would mark the end of the fall season and the readiness for the winter months.

His favorite time of year. Things became a bit crisper, clearer. Winter could be a cold wench to handle, but he enjoyed the challenge it brought. With winter came calm amongst the clans. No one liked or wanted to go out in the unpredictable snows to pillage and steal. Everyone stayed mostly to their own lands till the thaw of spring.

This was the time Christan honed his skills, recruited and trained new men, and enjoyed the comforts of a warm woman or two through the night, instead of having to draw up his pants and depart after the deed was done. He enjoyed the feel of a soft woman under him, but he enjoyed the comfort of her in his arms for hours afterward as well. Not that he'd admit that to anyone. He was ready to settle down, and soon he'd speak to Donovan about finding a wife. But not quite yet.

He had a mystery to solve. The New York woman. Christan pulled himself out of his chair and went in search of Devlin to report his findings and see if he knew anything of this woman. He didn't trust anyone else on the matter. Many would think him a bit loose in the head for talking about a woman vanishing like smoke. He couldn't have rumors milling about. He was the captain of the guard and had a certain image to keep.

He mounted the stairs, taking them two at a time to the third floor. The second floor was reserved for guests. The family took over the whole of the third floor. He reached the landing and took a right toward the rooms Devlin and Darrick occupied. The left wing was reserved for the laird and his family, and is where Donovan, his wife, Emily, and their young child resided. The large room facing the stairs was where their Mother's chambers were located. Being the matriarch of the family, she had the second to largest set of rooms, reaching out over the far wall of the keep. But Devlin and Darrick shared a wing, not that either of them needed a large set of rooms, being bachelors and all, so the two shared the large room at the end of the hall as a getaway when they needed peace and quiet. Their sleeping chambers faced each other along the hall. Each set of rooms identical, with a small setting room, the large bed chamber, and a dressing/bathing chamber. Simple in style, and completely adequate for their needs. If either one of them were to marry, the other would then move to the fourth floor turret until he too found a wife. Christan knocked briskly on Devlin's door.

"Enter," Devlin called

He walked into an empty sitting room. "Devlin, I have something I need to discuss." He closed the door and waited for Devlin to appear.

"Have a seat, ole friend. I'll join ye in a moment."

Christan took a chair facing the door, always on alert.

Devlin walked out, running his hands through his damp hair. "So what brings ye around? Did ye find anything on yer patrol?"

"That's why I am here. I found something a bit odd, though I am not sure I actually saw her."

Devlin's head snapped up "Her? Who are ye talking about?"

"Well, near the end of my patrol, I saw a woman, strangely garbed at the top of the east hill. She was just sitting in the heather and, when she heard me approach, she took off into the woods. I dismounted and followed her, catching her as she got to the little brook that runs through the eastern trees."

"So what did she say? Did ye bring her with ye? Where is she?" Devlin paced.

"She is gone. That's what I came to tell ye. I doubt if I even really saw her now. She felt real enough, and after I calmed her down she almost fainted on me, so I set her on the stones by the brook. After searching her for weapons of course."

At that statement, a low growl emanated from Devlin's throat, making Christan lean away a bit.

"And ye let her get away?" Devlin asked.

"No, she just disappeared. She was telling me where she was from and her eyes were making me a bit uncomfortable. I moved and the sunlight hit her face, then she was gone. Poof! Like magic," Christan explained.

"What?" Devlin stopped sharply and faced Christan.

"I have begun to think it was my imagination or a vision due to lack of food, but the way her body felt contradicts that theory."

Another low growl rose from Devlin. Advancing toward Christan, he said, "Well, if ye are having visions, then ye are sharing mine. I believe we have encountered the same woman."

Christan sat in silence. Devlin would share more in time. Prodding him would only incite his anger, and Christan planned to stay on his good side.

"I thought the stress was getting to me. When I was on patrol, I came upon whom I think is the same woman, sitting at the top of the hill in the east fields, just watching the keep and the herds. She seemed to be alone." Devlin sat on the sofa, facing Christan.

He ran his hands over his face. "I faded into the shadows of the trees to observe her and see if she posed a threat. She didn't move, just watched on in awe. I approached her from behind and asked who she was. She jumped and looked at me. The sun hit her face and she disappeared. I thought my mind might have been playing tricks on me, but I saw the gypsy's wagon heading toward the keep, so I headed to greet them, and that's when I sent ye out to finish my patrol."

Devlin glanced at Christan. "What do ye make of it?"

"I don't know, but I think we should increase the guard at the outer borders during the festival, just in case it's one of the O'Malleys tricks. I wouldn't put it past them to send a woman in disguise to throw us off," Christan advised.

"Aye, maybe ye are right. Send extra men to keep guard until the Festival is over. Let them know if they come upon this woman, to bring her straight to me, no matter when it is. I have to get to the bottom of this."

Christan nodded and stood. "I will assign the guard now."

Devlin relaxed. "Thank ye, Christan, and speak to no one of this until we figure out who she is. I shall see ye at evening meal."

"Till then." Christan bowed and backed out the door. Heading down the hallway, he came upon a page at the top of the stairs.

"Boy."

The page skidded to a stop "Yes, sire?"

"Go find Mycalos, Sean, and Gregor, and tell them to meet me at the gates."

"Yes, sire." The boy flew down the stairs to carry out Christan's orders.

Christan slowly made his way down the stairs and out the front door, heading to meet with his three elite guards. He'd set them on a rotating round of patrols. They'd be able to handle the waif of a girl if they should happen upon her. He studied the keep and saw Devlin watching him as he made his way to meet his men. He didn't blame Devlin. If he was half as shook up as Christan, all the trust in the world wouldn't keep him from making sure his wishes were carried out. He found the three men converging on the gate. It was time to give instructions and make ready for the rest of the visitors arriving this evening.

CHAPTER 8

Current Day

I glanced up from my e-reader and noticed the clouds had rolled in, turning the day from bright and sunny to drab and dreary. The manuscript I'd been reading just wasn't keeping my attention. If I had to force myself to read it, it wasn't worth passing on to the senior editors. I closed the cover and took my empty mug to the kitchen. Again, coffee didn't sound appealing. Hot chocolate sounded perfect this time of afternoon. I put some milk and a good dash of whipping cream in a pan to heat up. I didn't care for those little packets of instant mix you just added water to. I pulled down my secret stash of dark chocolates and opened the next cupboard to pull out my oversized mug specifically for hot cocoa. I rummaged through the utensil drawer, pulled out the grater, and set it next to the chocolate. I put the milk jug in the fridge and found my little package of mini milk-chocolate chips, then added them to the row of ingredients.

My phone rang as I shaved the dark chocolate into little wispy curls, preparing it for the warming milk. I scanned the caller ID. Mommy Dearest. I hit the ignore button and continued preparing the chocolate. The smell hitting my nose was heaven. My mouth started watering in anticipation of the smooth velvety taste of cocoa.

I set the spoon aside, put everything back in its place, rinsed out the grater, and set it in the sink. *Only one thing missing. I always keep a small jar of it stashed. Aha!* Top shelf of course. I pulled the jar down and added a large dollop of marshmallow cream to the top of the cocoa. A good mug of hot chocolate was all a girl needed on a dreary afternoon.

My phone rang again. I debated whether or not to answer, but it could be the publishing house, so I checked the caller ID. Todd's name popped up. I hit the answer button and put him on speaker as I walked into the alcove with my mug.

"Hey, what's up, Todd? Give me a sec. I have you on speaker, doll. My hands are a bit full right now."

"Oh oh, don't tell me you have a visitor," Todd snickered.

"No, you smart ass, but I do have the most decadent mug of hot cocoa, that is going to make me just as happy."

"Ugh, I should have known."

I took him off speaker. "There, that's better. What's up?"

"Much better. Now I wanted to make sure you got my email. I don't want any excuses for you not showing up Saturday."

"Yes, I got it and marked it on my day planner." I blew across the top of my cocoa, cooling it a bit. "I don't know what the big fuss is. I'm not out to impress anyone. I'm going to help raise money for those who need it, not to rub elbows with the rich and famous."

"You may not be, but I am, and I'm not walking into that place with you any less than your best. Think of it as your preparation for war. You need your war paint and your weapons cleaned and ready for battle."

"Todd, I'm not going into battle. If anything, I'm going to try staying in the shadows as much as possible. The less I have to interact with that woman, the better. And speaking of her, she called again today."

"What did she want this time?" Todd asked.

"I don't know. I didn't answer. I'm sure she left a lengthy voicemail for me. Reminding me of proper etiquette and how I should carry myself at the ball," I scoffed.

"Honey, you have more manners in your little finger than that wench does in her whole body. Don't you worry. You'll outshine her on Saturday. She'll be speechless. Just you wait."

"It'd feel good to knock her down a peg or two." I laughed.

"So, I'll see you Saturday morning? Or do I need to come get you?" Todd queried.

"I'll be up, but it may be easier if you pick me up. You can come here to finish getting ready, then we can just ride together. I'll make sure to chill a bottle of wine to enjoy before we go."

"Sounds good to me. I'll see you Saturday, doll. Have a great day, love you."

"Love you too, Todd. I couldn't do this without you," I admitted.

I closed my phone, picked up my mug with both hands, and inhaled. The cocoa had cooled enough to drink. Sipping slowly, I enjoyed the feel of the smooth chocolate as it made its way over my tongue and slid down my throat, wrapping me from the inside out in a cocoon of heat. I sat in my chair, staring out the window while I savored every last drop.

I grew tired as I sat there all cozy warm. I had nothing pressing to do today, so I opted to go take a nap, the second best thing to do on a gloomy afternoon. I took my mug to the kitchen, hoping the kitchen fairies would visit while I slept. A girl could hope, right?

My body knew what my plan was. It got sluggish as I pulled all the curtains closed and made my way to the bed. I snuggled in, not even taking the time to shed my clothing. It seemed too much of a task. I lay there, fully dressed under the covers. While turning over and plumping my pillow, my hand grazed the book I'd brought from the brook. I pulled it out and lay down on my side. I had yet to open it, a bit scared of what I might find inside. The design on the front again drew my attention, and I found myself tracing it with my fingertips. The cuff on my arm started to warm, and a sense of peace settled over me. I let my eyelids close, my hand still resting on the book. My last thought before succumbing to sleep was the keep.

I woke later to a burning sensation on my shoulder blade. I rolled onto my back, trying to shake the cobwebs of sleep from the corners of my mind. I sat up, still holding the book in my arms, then laid it on my lap. As soon as my hand left the cover, the burning in my shoulder stopped. Frowning, I reached around to feel my shoulder where the sensation had been, but nothing was out of the ordinary. I got up to check in the mirror. I saw nothing strange, no scratches or even reddening of the skin of my shoulder.

I gazed down at the book. "I wonder," I whispered as I reached down to touch the cover.

As soon as my fingers made contact, the burning sensation started, and I immediately removed my fingers. Confused, I tried it with both hands, but got no reaction, other than the feeling of calm filling me. Something was happening and I wanted to see. I took the book to the mirror with me. I set it on the counter, took my shirt off, positioned myself so that I could see my shoulder, and confirmed nothing was there. I then touched the cover with my fingers, never taking my eyes from the mirror. I gasped and dropped the book.

What the hell!

I saw a design, the same as the cover of the book, on my skin. I hurriedly picked the book up and touched it again. The burning returned and, the longer I kept touching it, the worse the burning became. I saw the design almost rising like a brand, the color seeming to dance under my skin. I held on as long as I could take the pain, before letting go. As soon as I released the book, the brand faded into the depths of my skin.

It was time to open this book up. I put my shirt on and went to the bed. Settled with my legs crossed, the book in front of me, I took a deep breath, closed my eyes, and opened the cover. I opened my eyes, and was greeted with a page full of script. I couldn't read it. It obviously wasn't written in English and, with my luck, it was probably written in some ancient tongue that died out a long time ago. I released the breath I'd held and shut the book again.

Well, that's not going to help me.

I glanced at the clock, and saw it was almost dinner time. I really needed to talk to someone, so I called Todd.

"No, you cannot get out of going tomorrow," he answered his phone.

"That's not why I'm calling."

"Oh, ok, what do ya need, doll?"

"Are you busy tonight? I thought we could have a dinner, whine, and gossip evening." I held my breath, hoping he didn't have plans.

"Well, I was thinking of checking out this new hot club down in the village," he teased. "But I could forgo that for a good evening of gossiping. What shall I pick up for dinner?"

I let out my breath. "How about Chinese?"

"You got it. I'll be over in thirty or so." He disconnected.

I headed into the kitchen, and took out a couple of plates and wine glasses, then set the bar. I had everything ready, so I sat down to wait, going over the events of the past hour in my head, and trying to figure out how to explain it all to Todd.

Twenty minutes later, I heard a knock on the door. I was in my room getting the book, so I yelled for him to come in. I walked into the kitchen to find him setting out the cartons of take-out.

He saw the book in my hands and raised his eyebrow in question. "New book?" he asked.

"Sort of. I'll explain after."

Todd dished out the food, and I poured the wine. We sat in comfortable silence, enjoying our dinner. That was one thing I loved about Todd. Whether we were chatting like magpies or simply being still in each other's company, he was happy. I swear, if he wasn't gay I'd have married him a long time ago. We finished up and I took our plates to the sink, setting them inside with my mug and grater from earlier. I cursed the kitchen fairies under my breath. They had yet again failed me.

Todd laughed at me. "I thought you would've learned by now that those fairies are fickle creatures. They have better things to do than wash your dishes."

"A girl can hope, right?" I smiled. "You grab the wine and I'll get the book. Let's head into the living room."

I switched on the lamps at either end of the couch and sat next to Todd, then placed the book on the coffee table and took my glass from him.

"So what's this gossip you have to share?" Todd inquired

I pulled the book to the edge of the table and opened it.

Todd leaned in, peering over my shoulder. "What language is that?"

"I don't know. I don't recognize it. But that's not the part you may think I'm crazy about." I closed the cover. "You see this design?"

"Yeah, Irish or Celtic right? Sort of familiar."

"It's very familiar." I took the cuff off my arm and set it next to the cover.

"Holy hell! It's exactly the same."

"Yeah, and wait till you hear the rest." I told him about what had happened earlier when I touched the book.

He flopped against the couch when I was done. "Can you show me?" he asked me with excitement in his eyes.

"I can try." I moved the cuff off the cover and set it on the table next to it. I pulled my sweatshirt over my head, then I maneuvered so he could see my shoulder from a better angle and lightly laid my fingers on the design.

Nothing.

"Where should I see it?" Todd asked.

"Right there on my shoulder blade, but I don't feel anything. It burned earlier when I touched it, as the design came to the surface, it got worse."

I withdrew my hand and faced him. "I don't understand. It happened three times today. I don't know why it won't do it now."

"Was there anything different when you did it earlier? Something you said or did?"

I shook my head feeling empty. My eyes settled on the cuff I'd removed and the emerald emitting a soft glow.

Todd followed my gaze and I heard his sharp intake of breath when he saw it.

We looked at each other. "The cuff."

I put the cuff on my arm and turned with the book in my lap so Todd could watch again. I laid my hand upon the book and immediately the burning started, more intense this time, the pain coming on faster. The cuff glowed brighter, warming my arm. The sides of the cuff started to conform to my arm and it scared me. I tried to take my hand away from the book, but found I couldn't. I was frozen in place.

Todd gasped behind me as the brand surfaced. The emerald glow was so bright that it bathed the room in a tint of green. Suddenly, the glow went out, my hand released from the book, and I slumped forward, trying to catch my breath. Todd's face was ashen when I glanced at him.

"Are you okay?" I shook him a little.

"That. Was. Amazing." He shook his head in disbelief. "Are you okay? I was worried for a second; you seemed to freeze and then that glow got brighter. It was a bit scary."

"I'm fine, a little tired. It went further this time, and my cuff got tight, and now I can't get it off." I tried to remove the band from my arm, but it wouldn't budge. I sat against the couch, then instantly sprang forward. My shoulder was on fire. I tried to see, but only glimpsed the edge.

I ran to the bathroom and noticed the brand staring at me smack dab in the middle of my shoulder blade, stretching down to just above my bra. The center was the same basic design as my cuff and the cover of the book, but around it was different knot work and vines or branches.

"What the hell is going on?" I looked up to find Todd in the doorway. "What is happening to me?" Tears erupted and flowed down my cheeks.

"I don't know, babe." Todd enveloped me in a hug, being careful not to touch the new brand on my shoulder. "But we'll figure it out. I promise. Right now, I think we could both use some sleep. We'll try to figure this out fresh in the morning."

I nodded against his chest.

He guided me from the bathroom and sat me down on the edge of my bed, then went to pull out one of my sleep shirts. Changing his mind, he put it down, and picked a tank top instead. He dressed me for bed and tucked me in, kissing my forehead. "Go to sleep, Jami."

My hand shot out to grasp his. "Don't leave me."

He squeezed my hand. "I won't; slide over and make some room."

I did as he asked. He slid down beside me and snuggled up, draping his arm over my stomach. I needed to feel safe and sane, and he'd help me stay grounded. I closed my eyes and let sleep overtake me.

CHAPTER 9

17th Century Scotland

"Jami, why are ye here?"

I didn't recognize where I was.

"I don't know. I must have been thinking about you when I drifted off to sleep."

I took in the small, round, wooden table, with a large candle burning in the center. We were in a small hut, the only light coming from the candle and from the fire at the end of the room. There was one small window covered with an animal fur situated above a bed, and a small wash stand in the far corner with a chipped water pitcher and bowl were the only other pieces of furniture in the room.

"Have a seat, Jami"

I turned to the table and realized Roma was sitting in the other seat, her long hair unbound and flowing around her shoulders. A peasant-style blouse and flowing skirt hid most of her body from sight, and her feet were bare. Looking down at myself, I found I was still in the tank and sweats Todd had put me in for bed.

I sat in the chair opposite her. "Roma, where am I?"

"First off, I think it's time to give ye my true name. I am Alexandria. Ye may call me Drea; all my friends and family do. Secondly, ye are in my dream. How ye got here I do not know, but it must be for a reason. Tell me what has happened."

I stared into Drea's stormy eyes and knew that anything I told her would stay between us. She'd believe me. Taking a deep breath, I twisted in my chair so she could see the brand on my shoulder.

Upon hearing her sharp intake of breath, I twisted back around. Her face had gone ashen, her eyes big pools, wider than I'd ever seen them. "It can't be." She shook her head. "My visions never foretold of this. My visions were very clear, but they didn't show me this."

She stood and started pacing the floor.

"What does it mean? I don't understand. Actually, I am really shaken up. I feel as if I am in a dream."

"That brand is no dream, Jami. When did it surface? What were ye doing?"

I explained to her about the book and cuff and everything that had happened.

Drea crouched next to me, running her fingers over the cuff attached to my arm. "And it won't come off ye say?" She traced the pattern woven into the metal, but avoided the emerald.

"No, it has shrunk to fit my upper arm and won't come off. If I try to remove it, the pain is intense and makes me sick. Drea, I'm scared."

"This book, have ye opened or read it?"

"I tried, but it's written in a language I don't recognize. "

"The book is for yer eyes only. Have ye tried to read it since the brand appeared?"

"No, I was so exhausted and confused so I went to bed. And here I am."

"Jami, ye need to read the book. Soon. I don't know all the answers ye are seeking. I only know what my visions have foretold. A woman, not of our time, will come with her knowledge and skill, so that this clan and all they hold dear will be saved from destruction. She is the soul mate to one of the brothers of the keep. It is her destiny to return to us. I don't know where she has been, but there is a legend of one who was whisked away and hidden in another time to protect her from the evil searching her out. It was told she would return one day and save us all."

"And you think this woman is me."

"Were ye raised by a family not of yer own blood? Were ye told at a certain age yer family was not yer own? And have ye been finding things that call to ye and ye can't explain how or why?"

I couldn't speak. She'd just described my life since my eighteenth birthday. Being told I was adopted, the box of things that sang to me, the brook, the leather-bound book, and now the brand and cuff. Everything was as she said. I shook my head in disbelief. It couldn't be. I was nothing special, and I couldn't save a whole family and their people.

Drea watched the door. "Jami, ye must go. Ye can't be found here."

"But this is a dream. No one can hurt us."

"There ye are wrong, just as ye have somehow found yer way to my dream; others can too." She glanced at the door again. "Go. Think of yer bed, yer time, yer world, and pull yerself out before they get here. I don't want them to know the wheels of fate are turning."

She ran over to my chair "Jami, go!"

She pushed me. My arms flailed out, trying to catch myself. The chair fell backwards, and I fell into blackness.

CHAPTER 10

Current Day

"Jami, Jami, wake up. You're dreaming." Todd shook me. I peeked up at him "That must have been some dream. You pack quite a punch." He rubbed his jaw where I must have hit him.

"Oh, Todd, I'm so sorry." I lightly touched his jaw.

"No big deal. I'm tough. What were you dreaming about?"

I tried to recall the dream, but only small bits came, then they were just out of reach.

"I'm not sure." I twisted my face in confusion.

"Well, no matter. We're up now. How about some coffee and breakfast?"

I nodded, still trying to pull the pieces of the dream to me. I knew something important had happened. I sighed in frustration and called out to Todd as he walked down the hallway. "Can you grab my book off the coffee table while you're out there?"

"Sure thing," he called to me.

I needed to try reading that book again.

I plumped all the pillows behind me, in no hurry to get out of bed, and sat waiting for Todd to bring my book. I didn't have to wait long. He brought my book and a steaming mug of coffee, which he placed on my nightstand. I beamed at him in thanks and positioned the book on my lap. He went to the kitchen to work on breakfast.

"We have a couple of hours before we have to head down to the spa for the day, so take your time, but don't get sucked in," Todd reminded me.

I'd forgotten about the spa. Two hours should be plenty of time. Hell, I couldn't read it the last time I opened the cover; what made me think I'd be able to now? A feeling. I took a sip of coffee and cradled the mug in my hands as I stared at the cover, willing it to sing or vibrate. I got no response. I set my mug down, then placed both hands flat on the leather, and felt an immediate jolt that grew into a slight hum of vibration against my hands.

"It's now or never, Jami." Breathing shallow in anticipation, I peeked at the first page, and the writing was no different. I still couldn't understand it. My shoulders fell in disappointment. I ran my fingers over the page, tracing a few of the characters and the cuff started humming. Right before my eyes, the characters swirled. My heartbeat picked up, my breathing became ragged, and slowly the characters settled into script on the page.

I could read it. I couldn't contain my excitement.

"Todd, hurry! Come here!" I squealed.

Todd quickly ran in. "What? What's wrong?" He searched frantically around the room.

I pointed at the book. "Look!"

Todd stared down at the page. "It's the same, Jami. I still can't read it. Did you figure out what dialect it is?"

"What?" I looked again and the words were there, plain as day. "The words changed, Todd, don't you see?"

He stared at me quizzically. "Are you saying you can read it?"

"Yes, I touched the page and my cuff started to hum, and then the characters started moving, and when they were done, I could read it. Plain English, right?" I was starting to get a bit scared. Couldn't he read it too?

"Honey, I still see the same thing I saw last night. But it seems like you don't. What does it say?"

I gazed down at the book, realizing only *I* understood what was written. I pulled the book toward me and started reading. What was written was unbelievable. It was a fable of sorts. Telling of a gypsy family blessed by the Fae in thanks for saving one of their own. One of the children from the gypsy family was allowed to marry into the Fae world. But they weren't allowed contact with their family outside of the Fae world afterward. They'd be taken to the Fae realm and live out their lives there. Not until 400 years had passed would any offspring be allowed into the human world. Each year the gypsy family and their descendants could visit in a neutral location, but only for a day, and only during the Harvest Festival when magic was at its highest. When the 400th year came, the child born would reenter the human world, but no memories were to be taken with the child. If the child lived till their twenty-fifth year, then, and only then, would their true heritage be revealed and their destiny unfold.

I flipped the page and found the next one blank. I flipped another and another to find the rest of the book blank.

That can't be all. Why would the book be so thick, if it only contained one story? I flipped back to the two pages I could read and noticed a small script at the bottom of the back of the last page. *Your destiny will be revealed on the hour of your birth, on the twenty-fifth year of your life.* I stared at the next page, still blank, but for just a moment it seemed to shimmer, revealing more text. I placed my hands on it, like the last time ... but nothing.

The hour of my birth. Eleven p.m. So does that mean I'll be able to see everything then? I checked the clock on my phone, even checking the date to make sure of myself. Yes, today was my birthday, which meant at eleven tonight, the rest of the text in the book would materialize on the pages.

I set the book aside, tossed the covers, and went in search of Todd. I found him in the kitchen finishing his breakfast. "I brought a tray back to you, but you seemed so engrossed in the book that I didn't want to disturb you."

"Thanks, I'm not that hungry anyway."

"So what does it say?"

I refilled my coffee, sat down, and filled him in on what I'd discovered.

Todd sat down.

I saw the wheels turning in his mind.

"So this will all happen while you are at the ball tonight? Should be interesting. Did it say what would happen?"

"No, it was all rather mysterious, just that my destiny would be revealed. I'm not sure I want to go now. I mean, I have no idea what's going to happen. Will I disappear, or turn into a fairy or what?"

"You aren't getting out of this that easy. Don't worry, I'll be by your side and, if anything weird starts to happen, I'll whisk you away and bring you here." Todd sat forward. "It will be okay. I don't know how, but deep down I know everything will be fine. We'll go to the party, you'll schmooze and get people to hand over twice what they planned, and then we'll come home and you can sit down and read that entire book of yours."

I wasn't sure, but thinking of the party didn't scare me, so I nodded in agreement. "Okay."

"Well then, go throw on some clothes and we'll head out. Our appointments start in about an hour. I'll clean this up and be done by the time you're ready."

I set my mug in the sink and headed down the hall to change.

CHAPTER 11

"You look absolutely stunning," Todd uttered.

I did a little twirl in front of him. The day of pampering had helped to calm me and build a little bit of excitement for the party. Todd always knew what I needed, and when I needed it. He'd been spot on with the dress. It fit like a glove. Paired with the shoes I did my best to not get drool on, and my jewels, I felt confident and invincible. My mother could say and do what she pleased tonight. It wouldn't get to me. I was above that.

"You picked some great armor for tonight. I can't thank you enough, Todd."

"Just enjoy yourself tonight. Don't worry about your mother. All eyes will be on you. I don't see how they couldn't be. You're radiant."

His words caused a warm blush to creep into my neck. Glancing at the clock in the kitchen, I saw it was eight p.m. "I suppose I've stalled enough. Let's go and get this over with. I have a book waiting for my return." I gazed longingly toward my bedroom, butterflies in my stomach. I didn't know what awaited me. I'd find out when we returned. I couldn't wait.

We walked outside to the limo Mother had sent over. She wanted to make sure I'd really come. Sitting in the plush leather interior, I let my mind wander, imagining what the book might reveal to me. What this destiny it spoke of could be.

I checked my bag to make sure I'd remembered the essentials: cell phone, lip gloss, ID, and money. I'd also put in the smaller envelope from my box. I planned to find a secluded spot at eleven p.m. to read it. I stroked the vellum for reassurance, then gazed out the window and watched the buildings go by.

When we arrived at the country club about forty-five minutes later, the driver held the door open, and Todd helped me out. Securing my hand in the crook of his arm, he gazed into my eyes. "Here we go, kid. Let's blow their socks off."

The ballroom was awe-inspiring. I expected nothing less from my mother. We were transported to another realm; one of glitter, snow and icicles, of magic and make-believe, of dreams and fairy dust. This wasn't what I'd expected. My mother wasn't the whimsical type, not one to believe in the possibilities of fairies and children's dreams. Large evergreens were placed around the floor, sprinkled with glitter and just a hint of snow. Each pillar was encased in ice and glittery lights. Candles were strategically placed, giving off a warm, welcoming glow. No harsh overhead lights penetrated the magical ambiance. I was impressed. Something clicked inside me and I knew that I was home. It truly scared me. I could never feel this way about something my so-called mother created, but I tried to get past my head and listen to my heart.

"I'll go grab us a drink." Todd left me to mingle a bit.

I saw the director from the children's wing at the hospital and went to greet him. I pasted a smile on my face, stood a bit straighter, and continued on, answering greetings called out, shaking hands, and returning hugs. It was expected. As I made my way through the ball room, I noticed my mother. I inclined my head at her wave, and twisted to go the other way. I wasn't ready to speak with her yet. A small bench huddled in between a couple of evergreens called my name. I sat and waited for Todd to return with our drinks. A nip of courage was needed before I continued on with the night. I didn't see any sign of Todd as I settled down and relaxed. As my back hit the cushions of the bench, I smelled the evergreens, and a sense of peace enveloped me. I just needed to escape for a bit. I really didn't like crowds, even for a short period of time. The branches shook and seemed to close in around me, sheltering me from the people on the floor. I closed my eyes and sent them a silent thank you. The cuff on my arm warmed and my necklace hummed.

That was how Todd found me, with my eyes closed and a smile

on my face. "I don't know what you are doing, but you might want to stop."

I cocked my head to the side. "Why?"

He pointed to my necklace. The center emerald glowed. I gasped and sat up. The glow faded as my senses came down to earth.

"What are you doing hidden in here? I almost missed you. If it weren't for the train of your dress, I would have walked right past."

"That was the idea. I needed to hide for a minute, to catch my breath." I took my champagne glass from his hands.

"Your mother asked for you."

I sighed. "I suppose I can't hide from her all night." I took the hand Todd offered. "Let's go see what she wants."

Todd escorted me over to my mother. She was in a deep discussion and didn't notice my approach. Todd cleared his throat to get her attention.

"Jami! I'm so glad you came. We have so much to catch up on." She hugged me. "Why aren't you answering my calls, dear?" she whispered in my ear before letting go.

"Good evening, Mother. You're very lovely tonight."

"No need to be so formal, Jami," my mother chided. "And, Todd, don't you look dashing tonight?" She air kissed his cheeks.

"Thank you, Mrs. Morgan, always a pleasure to see you."

"Now, Jami, there are some people I'd like you to meet." She grabbed my arm and proceeded to walk me around the room, introducing me to all the people she thought were influential. Showing me off like a prized pooch, rather than a beloved daughter. This was my mother's way: emotionally unattached, using what she had to gain respect in other's eyes. She'd hid it well while I grew up, but I recognized her now for what she was. Using me as a way to climb the social ladder even higher.

"Yes, we're so proud of Jami and her decision to go out and make a name for herself. Not relying on the family money to make it in this world," she said as I tuned into the conversation.

I barely stopped my eyes from rolling. What a load of hogwash.

"Jami, dear, I'm getting a bit parched. Could you run and grab me a glass of champagne? I don't know where all the waiters have run off to," Mother said.

"Of course. I'll be right back," I gagged out.

Relief washed over me as I walked away. I found a waiter carrying a tray laden with flutes of champagne. I grabbed one, and directed him over to where my mother held court. I made my way to the doors we'd come through when we arrived, then looked down the hall, searching for a place to hide out for a bit. I was getting a bit claustrophobic in the ballroom with all the people milling about.

A darkened hallway to the right looked promising. No lights meant no people, or those only involved with themselves and their partners. I found a small library at the end of the hall empty. I quietly snuck in and closed the door behind me, then made my way over to an overstuffed chair situated by one of the long windows. I sat and just breathed for a minute. I took my phone out of my purse and texted Todd, "Hiding out for a bit, don't worry if you don't see me. Will catch up with u." Leaning my head against the chair, I closed my eyes. The hum of my jewels started, and a feeling of peace came over me as I focused on my breathing, and the sounds and smells of the room around me. I peeked out the window, then down at my hands to find I was stroking the clutch I'd brought. I opened it to get my compact, and the envelope fluttered out. I checked my phone quickly. 10:50 p.m. I set my clutch and phone on the table beside me and, with shaky hands, gently opened the flap on the envelope.

A picture floated out into my lap. I set the letter aside and picked up the picture. It was a young couple, smiling happily at the camera. The woman was round with child and they were standing in front of the ruins of what appeared to be a castle. They seemed to be excited about where they were. I took a closer look and realized I recognized the wall they were standing in front of. It was the same wall of the keep I'd dreamt about. The air in the library grew thicker the longer I stared at the picture. My jewels started to glow and the cuff on my arm was warmer. I needed to read the next letter. I knew it in my bones. I set the picture aside and picked it up. I held my breath as I unfolded it, then read:

My dear Jami,

How I miss you. I know I have only just left you. I already miss you with every bone in my body. That is not why I write to you. It is time you know your destiny. You are meant for a greater purpose. Your father and I put you with the Morgans to keep you safe. It was the only way to ensure you would grow to your maturity and fulfill the visions I have seen. You will be our saving grace, if you only read on with an open mind.

Many years ago, it was foretold of a young woman who would travel from afar to us. A woman who would capture the heart of a man that could destroy the only life we know. You may have been having dreams or visions of this man before now, but know he is your destiny. He is your soul mate and, if the prophecy isn't fulfilled, his heart will turn black and he will destroy his family and people in his strife for revenge. You, dear Jami, are that woman. My visions told me the day you were born.

You see, we are descendants of the O'Malley clan, but were cast out because of something that happened years ago, and we are not recognized by the family. Our ancestors were welcomed into a family of gypsies, and we have traveled and lived with them ever since. They taught us to embrace our gifts, to love the land, and how to live our lives to the fullest without pain and regret. We have Fae blood running through our veins, and it is that blood that provides us with the gifts we have. Each child's gifts are unknown until they reach the age of maturity. The age of twenty-five. My gift was that of sight. It was thanks to this gift I was able to whisk you away to safety. I made a deal with our Fae family to keep you safe, but in doing so, I would never get to see you again. For that, I am sorry, dear Jami. I wasn't there to raise you and teach you all I know. I only hope you can forgive me.

I placed a couple of items to find you when the time was right. If they have found their way to you, I am sure they will teach and guide you as I was not able to. Your jewels, these you must keep with you at all times. They are part of you. They will help lead you in the right direction, down the right path. Those jewels are a gift from your Fae line. The book of Cranaugh is the other piece of the puzzle I hope has found you. I wrote down our complete history and the visions I had. Keep this book with you as well. It will guide you to where you need to go and what you need to do.

You are our pride and joy, Jami. We only want the best for you, and I know if you follow your path, not only will you save the family, but you will find true love in the process. That is all I wish for you, to live a long and happy life with the one you love.

So, Jami, if you are ready, on the striking of the hour of your birth, in the twenty-fifth year of your life, recite the following words and all will be revealed to you:

"Here and now, on the hour of my birth, on the twenty-fifth year of my life, I am ready to receive my destiny. Fates open up and show me the way."

Jami, remember I will always love you.

I set the letter down and gazed out the window, trying to grasp what I'd just read. Was I ready to take the leap and see if this was real? I checked the screen on my phone to see it read 10:58 p.m. Should I text Todd? No, if I was going to do this, it had to be just me. The brand on my shoulder pulsed and itched. I wanted to reach around and scratch it, but didn't. I didn't have much time to decide what to do. The jewels at my neck and around my arm started humming and glowing. There was a cloud covering the moon as I stared out the window.

I was scared. What would happen? Would anything really happen? I only had about a minute to decide and, as I gazed up to the sky, the clouds cleared from the moon and the grandfather clock behind me struck eleven. The jewels glowed brightly, and I returned my eyes to the letter, then took a deep breath.

"Here and now, on the hour of my birth, on the twenty-fifth year of my life, I am ready to receive my destiny. Fates open up and show me the way."

The brand on my shoulder, the cuff on my arm, and the necklace at my throat all burned at the same time with an intense heat. I was blinded by the light radiating from the emeralds. My head fell hard against the chair and my body sagged, as though my veins were filling with lead. I couldn't move a muscle. I tried to get up and, as the glow got brighter in the room, blackness overtook me.

I woke to find myself lying in the field of heather. I stood and brushed off my skirt and, noticing I was at the field, glanced down to find myself garbed in a simple dress. My feet were encased in soft-leather slippers. I reached up to find my hair in one long braid with a piece of cloth tied around it. I glanced around to see if anyone had noticed me. From the sound of it, everyone was within the walls of the keep. Music and loud cheers came from inside, and I saw the smoke from what I imagined was a large bonfire.

Off to my right was the camp Alexandria had told me was her family's. It seemed safest to venture over there. I made my way through the heather, but when I got there, the fire was cold and there was no one around. Unsure of what to do next, I sat on the logs positioned around the cold fire. I sat for a little while, trying to decide what to do. I didn't know how I'd gotten there, or if I really was there, or if this was simply another one of my dreams. Suddenly, I noticed the sound of bells and laughter approaching.

I searched for a place to hide, but wasn't quick enough.

Alexandria ran up to the camp with a younger woman. She stopped quickly when she saw me. She whispered something to the woman with her and spun her to go down toward the keep. I should have been afraid, but I wasn't. When Alexandria twisted back around, I noticed she had a cuff on her arm similar to mine, and it was glowing. Only hers was an amethyst instead of an emerald.

"Alexandria?"

She walked over and sat next to me. "It's yer birthday, isn't it, Jami?"

I nodded.

With a sigh, she took my hand. "I had hoped to have a little more time to prepare ye." Looking up at the sky, she said, "The fates have other plans." She stood, pulling on my hand. "Come then, it's time to introduce ye."

I stood, but didn't move forward. "Alexandria, am I really here, or is this just another dream?"

Before she could answer, the young woman came racing up to us. "Drea, father says to bring her at once. It's no longer safe outside the keep walls."

We took a step and I heard the most horrendous scream behind us. We both slowly turned to see a line of men on horseback, with torches in their hands, barreling down the hill toward the keep.

Alexandria took off at a run, pulling me behind her. "Hurry, we must get inside the walls now!"

I followed as fast as I could and, just as we reached the castle walls, there was a sting in my calf. I fell and lay there stunned for a moment, before strong arms picked me up and carried me the rest of the way. I stared at my leg, at the arrow sticking out of it, and a stream of blood trailing from the wound. I promptly blacked out.

When next I awoke, I found myself in the library again, and a feeling of nausea overtook me. I swallowed to keep it at bay. I couldn't go to the party. I was sweating and my leg hurt like a bitch. I sent Todd a text, "Need to go home now, come find me in the library."

I sat waiting for Todd, breathing through the nausea. I gathered my letter, which had fluttered to the floor, and placed it and the picture into my clutch. I heard a knock on the door as it cracked open. Todd's head peaked around. Seeing me, he moved the rest of the way in. One look at my face had him at my side.

"Jami, what happened? Are you okay?"

"I need to go home. I need to get to the book. I'll explain later, just get me out of here."

He helped me out to the hallway. "Take a right. There is a door out the side we can take."

As soon as we were outside, Todd found a valet taking a quick smoke break and instructed him to inform the driver we were ready to go home. The valet did as he was told.

Todd helped me around front just as the car pulled up. The driver quickly got out to assist in getting me into the rear seat. The door shut and Todd asked, "It happened, didn't it? Why didn't you call for me? Dammit, Jami, someone should have been with you." He stared out the window as the car drove away.

"I'm sorry. I had to do this on my own." The nausea was lessening, but the pain in my leg wasn't. Todd's leg brushed against mine and I sucked in a breath, my face contorted with pain.

"What's wrong? Let me see." He didn't wait for an answer. He lifted the skirt of my dress to see a large area on my leg inflamed and angry looking. "What the hell?"

"I can't explain it. I need to get to the book. I have to get back."

"Okay, okay, we'll be there soon." He wrapped his arm around my shoulders and, being careful of my leg, pulled me into his side. "Just relax, Jami, it'll be all right." He didn't sound convinced, but didn't say anything when he felt me crying against his chest. He rubbed my shoulders until we reached my apartment building.

The car pulled up outside my building. Todd didn't wait for the driver to open the door; he just jumped out and picked me up "Todd, I can walk." I laughed. Yet he insisted on carrying me to the elevator.

"No, you can't, not until I can take a better look at that leg. What happened? You can tell me, you know."

"I'm not sure I can. I don't know how to explain it. I read my birth mother's letter, which gave me instructions on how to reveal my destiny that the book spoke of. It just seemed right to say the words, so I did, and then I was transported to another place and time.

I was talking to someone and we were attacked. I was running to safety when I felt a sharp pain in my leg, then I woke up in the library and sent you the text."

Todd helped me to the apartment and carried me to my bed. He set me down gently and looked at my leg. "It doesn't seem nearly as bad as it did in the car."

I tested it out, flexing my foot to move the muscle, and he was right. It didn't hurt nearly as bad. Just a faint twinge. I glanced down to see the skin was a faint shade of pink.

I sat up and pulled the book out from underneath my pillows. "I think it's time to learn more about this destiny of mine."

Todd went to get the wine, and I opened the first pages. This time when I paged through the book, it was full of text.

Todd handed me my glass.

"Are you ready?"

"Whenever you are." He climbed onto the bed with me and made himself at home. We settled in and I started reading, feeling a sense of calm having Todd lying next to me.

CHAPTER 12

17th Century Scotland

It was Saturday and the Festival was in full swing. All the clansmen, friends, and family from far and wide had gathered to celebrate this bountiful Fall Harvest. Musicians set up all throughout the bailey. The children ran around playing games. The kegs of ale had been tapped earlier in the day and would keep flowing as the day progressed. A great bonfire was planned for the evening, and a meal to outdo all others would be set up in the keep. The tables had been removed from the great hall to make room for dancing.

Devlin surveyed the hustle and bustle as he descended the stairs outside. He had to check up on the guard to make sure the ramparts and outer borders were being patrolled. He'd have Christan get the rotating patrols ready so all the men could participate in the festival throughout the day. Not only was Christan the head of Devlin's guard, but his best friend since childhood

"Good morning, sir," one of his guards greeted him.

"Good day, McKinney, have ye seen Christan around?"

"I saw him up in the lists early this morning, sir, but not since."

"Very well, then. If ye see him about, tell him I have need of him," Devlin said, dismissing the guard.

"Yes, sir." McKinney went about his duties.

Devlin loved this time of year. He loved to see the children play, so light at heart, with so much yet to come in their lives. He enjoyed watching the people of his clan celebrate and rejoice in the hard work they'd done. They had earned the break. This was a tough life to live, not many joys to celebrate, and they all needed this Festival.

He continued through the courtyard, nodding at the warriors he came upon, making sure all posts were manned. Even though today was one for celebration, they could never let their guard down completely. This was still a time of strife, each clan warring against another for some stupid reason. He didn't understand why they couldn't work together for a common goal. He'd done research on the lands adjoining theirs. Their lands were rich in soil and prime for crops, but they had very few fields that were adequate for their herds to graze upon. The O'Malleys had higher grounds, not optimal for crops, but they were ideal for grazing. If he could only get his brother to see that by working out a truce agreement, both clans would benefit. If they could move their herds to the O'Malley lands it'd free up four more fields for planting. In exchange for the grazing rights on the O'Malley lands, he proposed giving them the planting and harvesting rights to those four fields. But no, his brother didn't want to hear it. In his eyes, there could be no peace with the O'Malleys.

Devlin shook his head as he continued walking on. His brother never listened to him. If they didn't come to some agreement soon, the O'Malleys would hit again. Hell, this feud was the reason they'd sent their sister away to live with an aunt in the city. If the feud ended, Iona could return. He missed her. She was the youngest in the family and could always brighten a room with just her smile. If Devlin knew his sister, she'd show up soon. Donovan forbade her to attend the Festival, but she had a mind of her own, and if she were to just show up, their eldest brother, laird of the clan, couldn't turn her away. So he expected to see her carriage arrive at any moment.

Devlin strode out the gates, taking a quick walk around the walls to make sure everything was secure and the guards posted were both awake and sober. Seeing that things were in order, he walked around the interior walls of the keep, and heard the ring of broadswords. He stepped through the back gate and stopped to observe the men of the clan going up against each other, testing their skills with broadswords in the lists. Devlin veered off the path and went to watch. They were always in search of good strong men to join the guard. This was a good time to see who among them had the natural talent needed to wield the heavy broadswords they carried.

He found Christan.

"Ah, the great Devlin decides to grace us with his presence," Christan greeted him, smiling. "I did not expect to see ye out here today, with so much to be done at the keep."

"Och, Donovan and Emily have that well in hand. I would have simply been in the way."

"I see, so ye snuck out before Lady Emily could put ye to work." Christan laughed.

"Of course, she has plenty of maids and servants to do her bidding. My expertise is needed elsewhere."

"Anywhere she is not, I assume."

"Exactly," Devlin said, giving Christan a good slap on the shoulder. "So do we have any promising young lads this year?"

"Aye, there are a few. Young Galin and Sebastian are both talented with a broadsword and in hand-to-hand combat. I would suggest we have a sit down with them and their dad soon. Their talents would be put to better use in the guard than out in the fields."

"Very well; we will do so after the celebration." "Sir Christan, Lord Devlin, are ye here to show us how it should be done?" a young lad called out.

Devlin turned to Christan. "Well, ole friend, what say ye? Shall we show these young lads how it's done?"

Christan bowed to Devlin. "After ye, *old* friend." Devlin removed his over cape and accepted the broadsword the squire handed him. He tested the weight in his hands and headed to the middle of the lists, where he warmed up with a few practice strokes and defensive moves. Christan did the same, coming up to stand across from him.

"So how shall we play this one? First unarmed, or first blood?" Christan asked.

"Ye have to ask? Always first blood, my friend." Devlin attacked, taking Christan off guard.

Christan backed up, getting a better stance, and deflecting the blows Devlin delivered. They circled each other, watching for any opening or weakness the other would reveal. They continued to parry back and forth for ages. Both worked up a good sweat, but neither showed signs of fatigue. The sounds of swords clashing rang through the valley as they both realized this wasn't just a typical practice session.

Devlin could tell the moment Christan's efforts changed. He stopped holding back and went from fun sword play to a true fight. That was fine with Devlin; he would take out his frustrations and pent-up energy on the field.

Devlin matched Christan swing for swing, until Christan stepped over a rock and faltered just a fraction. It was enough for Devlin to strike in and slice his upper arm. Christan laid his broadsword down, conceding defeat. Applause broke out amongst the men and women watching. Devlin grinned and grasped Christan's forearm. "Good battle, friend. I hadn't realized how much I needed that."

"My pleasure. Now I must find some pretty maid to help tend to this wound ye have inflicted upon me." Christan strode toward the keep with a wicked grin on his face.

Devlin grabbed his over cape and continued his walk of the perimeter. He reached the far side where the rock jutted out over the water. Stopping, he let the strong breeze cool and dry the sweat from his battle and clear the cobwebs from his mind. More and more, he found himself wondering about the waif of a girl he'd seen sitting on the hill. He had yet to find her, but knew she would return. He didn't know how, but she would. And when she returned, it wouldn't be good.

Devlin noticed the sun had made its way past the noon mark. He didn't know how long he and Christan had battled, but his stomach reminded him he'd missed the noon meal. He headed toward the keep. Hopefully he could sweet-talk some cold meat and cheeses out of the kitchen maids.

Christan found Devlin sitting on one of the large tree stumps that had been brought in and situated around the pyre of wood for the bonfire later that night.

"Ye seem a bit happier than when I saw ye earlier," Christan commented.

"A full belly and flagon of ale will do that to a man." Devlin raised his mug in greeting.

"Do ye want to tell me what is bothering ye? That wasn't just some practice swordsmanship earlier. Ye were out for blood. I am only glad ye stopped at the scratch on my arm." Christan sat down next to his lifelong friend.

"Och, I don't know what's wrong with me. Every time I turn around, I am thinking about that damn woman. I can't seem to get her out of my mind, and my gut tells me she'll come again ... and soon."

"Ah, I wondered if she might have something to do with it. The patrols haven't seen hide nor hair of her. It's like she vanished."

"I know; that's what bothers me. I can't place her with any of the families near us. But it seems the gypsy sister may know her, which means she could hail from almost any part of the country," Devlin said, staring into his ale.

"Have ye spoken to the sister?"

"Nay, my sister-in-law has had her squired away up in her chambers since they arrived. I haven't seen the gypsy without Emily right next to her."

"Ah, I can see where that would prove to be a problem. Maybe later tonight during the festivities ye can sneak her away and ask her what she knows," Christan suggested.

"I just may do that." Devlin gazed up to the sky, gauging the time. "Almost time to get the bonfire going. What say ye, Christan? Ye up for helping get this thing roaring?" Devlin asked mischievously.

"Ye don't have to ask me twice." They each went to grab one of the torches placed throughout the courtyard to light the pathways, and brought them to the pyre, taking opposite sides. They started the kindling aflame, and had a strong blaze going, then stood to the side to watch it slowly climb the pyre.

It was then they heard a young lass screaming. "Attack! We are under attack!"

Devlin and Christan threw their torches into the fire and took off for the gate. "Close the gate, man the wall, men to arms!" Christan veered right to get the archers set about the parapet of the wall.

Devlin drove straight for the gate, helping to close it.

The young lass was there. "Wait! Wait; my sister and her friend are still out there. We can't leave them."

Devlin peered out through the crack of the gate to see two young women running toward them. "Hold the gates!" He wouldn't leave anyone outside the safety of the walls.

At that moment, he saw their faces and his breath left him in a whoosh. It was her. She was here. Jami glanced up and met Devlin's eyes before she fell. Devlin took off the moment he saw her falter.

Running past the gypsy, he scooped the woman into his arms. "Run, lass, get to the keep," he bellowed as he ran past her to the gates. Drea was right behind him as he passed through. He carried the strange woman up to the house, shouldering his way through the door. She was in shock, but still conscious, or so he thought.

Emily met them at the door and guided them to her private sewing atrium on the ground floor, setting the stranger on the sofa where she promptly passed out and disappeared.

Devlin's steps faltered in shock.

"Close the doors, Emily. Quickly," Drea instructed.

"I must get to the gates," Devlin said

"No, ye must stay here, Devlin. It was only a small band, maybe eight or ten men. Yer guard will dispatch of them quickly enough without yer help. I need ye here," Drea pleaded, her eyes going stormy with knowledge.

Emily closed the doors. "Is it time already, Drea? I thought ye said it wouldn't be till the end of the Festival."

Drea glanced at Emily. "My visions do not always tell me the exact time. I saw it was to be the end of the Festival, but I was wrong. Today is her birthday, not Monday as I had thought."

"Oh my, and she's hurt. How? When?" Emily couldn't get the questions out fast enough.

"I don't know. She must have returned home, but as for her

injuries, I believe she was shot as we ran to the gate," Drea said.

Devlin stood and listened, confusion and frustration overtaking him. "What in the hell are ye two talking about?"

Emily sat. "Devlin, sit down. It's a long story and it seems that we have the time to tell it. We don't know when she will return, but I think ye need to know of Drea's visions as they include ye."

Devlin looked between Emily and Drea before he spoke again. "Visions? That's hogwash. I don't put any faith in visions."

Emily tsked him. "Ye should. Yer father put his faith in her father's visions, and she has the same gift, only hers are more accurate and more detailed. Please, for me. Just sit and listen."

He wouldn't make it out of Emily's sewing room anytime soon if he didn't concede. He picked the least feminine chair in the room and plopped down. "Can I at least have a drink while ye spin yer tales?"

"Of course." Emily filled a flagon with ale from the pitcher by the mantle. Handing it to Devlin, she indicated that Drea speak. "Why don't ye tell him all ye know?"

Drea took a deep breath. "About two weeks ago, I started having the visions. They were more like dreams that foretold of a woman who would come from another land and time. She would play a big part in the future of this clan. She is the descendant of the O'Malleys, but she is different. She comes from the line taken by the Fae two hundred years ago."

"That's just a fairy tale," Devlin interrupted.

"So many think, but I am telling ye that fairy tale is actually true. She carries the blood of the Fae in her veins, along with that of the O'Malleys. On her twenty-fifth birthday, she will be shown her destiny, and if she chooses, she will come here to either save yer clan or destroy it."

"This is a bunch of bull—"

Emily cleared her throat.

"The O'Malleys don't live anywhere near us. The Mulligans pretty much wiped them out in the last feud."

"Her clan is still alive and well, just spread over the country. She will be the one to bring them if she accepts her destiny. She will unite the O'Malleys and the O'Rorkes and only does this with yer help, Devlin. Ye see, her destiny is intertwined with yers."

Drea paused to catch her breath. Glancing to Emily for support, she continued, "When Jami comes, she is going to be confused, scared, and will need all the support she can get. I will be here to help her, as will Emily."

Emily nodded. "Devlin, I have asked Drea to stay on after the Festival. I think Jami will need her."

"I have had enough of this. Ye have let this fraud swindle ye, Emily." Devin stormed out of his chair. "I have to get to my men."

"If ye choose to help her, Devlin, she will bear ye a son in the future. If ye don't, then ye will watch as yer whole family is destroyed," Drea said to his back as he walked out the doors.

CHAPTER 13

Current Day

I'd been reading in the book for a while when I stopped to take a breath and a drink of my wine. Todd had gotten up at some point during my reading and fetched a chilled bottle from the fridge. He was twirling his glass with a far-off look in his eyes.

"What are you thinking?" Jami inquired.

"I'm thinking I may lose you through this, and I don't know what I'll do without you in my life," he answered.

"Oh, Todd, I have no idea what this means, but I'm not leaving you. I'll figure out how to keep you with me somehow."

"We'll see, darling. Keep reading. I know you want to figure it all out. Don't mind me." He snuggled down next to me, curling up under the comforter.

I continued reading. So much information, and I didn't understand any of it. I flipped through the pages, searching for how to go back to Drea and the clan. There was unfinished business there, and I had so many more questions for her.

My eyes grew heavy and I needed to get out of this dress. I set the book aside, and quietly got up and went to change. After shedding the night's armor, I felt more like myself again. I went and picked the book up. As I laid it on my lap, it fell open to a spell of some sort. As I read further, I realized I'd found exactly what I was searching for. I glanced at Todd sleeping next to me. "I'll be back soon, I promise," I whispered.

I leaned over and kissed him, took the book out to my chair, and read the passage three times to make sure I had it right.

I closed my eyes and recited the phrases I'd found, picturing Drea in my mind. Everything went foggy and I became weightless, as if I was floating. As the fog cleared, the pain set in. It was like someone was trying to hack off my lower leg. I tried to open my eyes, then a searing pain brought me to a sitting position, and I promptly blacked out again.

CHAPTER 14

17th Century Scotland

When I finally did come to, Drea sat across from me with just the light of the fire to brighten the room. I tried to roll over, and immediately stopped when pain shot up my leg. Drea got up and brought me a glass of water. "Here, drink this. Ye need it." She brought the cup to my lips.

"Thank you," I said, lowering my head to the pillow.

"Yer welcome. I am sorry about the pain, we couldn't give ye anything until ye woke up. The healer has been and gone. He did his best to remove the arrow and patch yer wound. The drink I gave ye has a bit of laudanum in it; that should help not only with the pain, but sleep."

At that moment, a monster stood and laid its head on my stomach, staring at me with puppy-dog eyes and a wagging tail. I couldn't help but pet him. "And who do we have here?"

"He has lain at yer side since ye returned. I feel he has decided ye are to be his master," Drea said with a smile. "I am told he hasn't responded to any of the trainers and he has been deemed useless. But I think he has been waiting for ye."

I stared into his eyes. "Hmm, you're a bit of a scruffy monster, aren't you?" I focused on Drea. "What is his name?"

"He has no name."

Gazing into his eyes, I said, "No name, eh? We can't have that." I looked at Drea. "What breed is he?"

"He is a wolfhound. The O'Rorkes breed them for hunting and protection."

"Ah, I should have guessed. Well, we need a name that lives up to your handsomeness. How does Argus sound?" The hound barked twice and promptly licked my face. I wiped at the doggy slobber, laughing.

"I think he approves. If ye are up to it, Emily has prepared a room for ye. It is upstairs. I will get someone to carry ye if ye are ready."

"I don't need to be carried. I have one good leg. With a bit of help, I can make it. Just give me a few minutes."

Drea helped me to sit, gave me more water, then helped me to stand.

"I really think I should get one of the men to help us." A worried look crossed her face.

"I've never had to depend on a man before. I'm not going to start now."

We slowly made our way to the stairs. I was sweating by the time we reached the bottom. While gaping at the many steps, my vision suddenly clouded and I saw stars. Breathing deeply, I went to take the first step, leaning heavily on Drea. She was winded, but didn't say anything.

"What the hell are ye doing?"

I glanced over my shoulder to see who'd bellowed at us. Standing a few feet behind us was the man I saw the first time I visited in my dreams. "I'm going to my room," I responded.

"Like hell. Ye won't make it half way."

Before I could answer, he scooped me up and took the stairs two at a time. Drea rushed to keep up with him. He reached the landing and, instead of setting me down, he continued to carry me down the hall to a large door. He opened it with a shove of his boot, carried me over to the bed, and put me down. "I don't want to see ye trying to walk around until yer leg is healed. I don't need ye falling down and injuring yerself further."

He twisted to walk out, tripping over Argus who was racing in to catch up. "Damn dog should be outside. Useless mutt," he grumbled.

After he left, Drea walked in.

"Who was that?" I asked.

"That was Devlin, middle brother in the Clan O'Rourke."

"He's a jackass."

"I suppose he can be. Don't worry about him right now. Let's get ye ready for bed. Emily put a few things in here, thinking ye may not have any change of clothes with ye."

I fingered the blood-stained gown I had on. "No, I don't."

After getting washed up and dressed in a borrowed night gown, Drea helped me to bed. I was exhausted from the trek to my new chambers.

"Just lie down and rest, Jami. We have plenty of time to talk tomorrow."

Argus jumped up onto the bed, curling up at my feet. "Argus there has decided he's staying, so sleep tight." As she reached the door, she glanced over her shoulder. "If ye need anything before morning, tell Argus to find me."

I nodded, half asleep as she closed my door.

I woke up a few hours later, really needing to pee. I realized then that I hadn't seen any bathrooms in the manor. Argus sat up the moment I moved. He stared at me with his tail wagging, waiting for instructions. Drea had said to tell him to find her, but he really couldn't understand me, could he? It was worth a try. I really had to go. "Argus, find Drea."

He hopped off the bed, pranced over to the door, sat, looked over his shoulder, and then nosed the latch open. Using his teeth, he pulled the door handle and walked out. I heard his toenails clacking on the stone floor as he ran down the hallway. Within minutes, he returned with Drea. My jaw dropped as they both walked in. "He really did understand me. That's amazing."

Drea nodded. "I thought he would. What can I help ye with?"

My face heated. "I didn't see a bathroom on my way up."

"Of course; I should have thought of that. Here, let me help ye behind the screen."

"The what?"

Drea nodded to the corner where a screen had been placed. "It's right over there. It's actually really nice, with a seat and everything. It's one of the reasons Emily put ye in this room. She knew ye wouldn't be able to support yerself. When ye're done, I'll take care of it."

I couldn't believe this. No bathroom, just a pot. How unsanitary. I didn't know if I could do it, but my bladder decided for me. I nodded and Drea helped me do what was necessary, then got me into bed. I was so embarrassed. She tucked me under the covers and fluffed my pillows. "Would ye like me to stay? I can have a pallet brought in."

Glancing around the room, I said, "Yes, I'd like you to stay, but this bed is big and has plenty of room. We can share it."

Argus let out a low growl.

"I am not sure Argus agrees. It will take no time to have a pallet brought in."

"No, Argus, it's fine. She's the only friend I have besides you, and we can share the bed."

He lowered his head onto his paws.

"See? No issue; Climb on in."

She pulled down the covers and climbed in, settling herself on the far side of the bed. She rolled to her side. "Are ye doing alright?'

"I'm doing as well as can be expected, considering I've traveled back in time, found out I'm the key to saving or destroying a family, been shot in the leg with an arrow, and peed in a bowl." I laid my head on the pillow. "I don't know what I'm doing, Drea. I'm so confused and every time I try to figure it out, my head hurts."

"Then follow yer heart; learn to trust in yer instincts. I know it's a lot to take in, and I am here to help in any way I can." Drea reached out to squeeze my hand. "For now, let's try to get some rest. Tomorrow is going to be a big day."

I squeezed her hand in companionship. "Sleep well."

I snuggled down under the blankets and furs, taking care to not move my leg much. Argus moved up to lie against my side and give me some added warmth. I closed my eyes and willed myself to sleep, thinking of Todd and all the things I wanted to tell him.

I found myself standing in my bedroom, Todd sleeping soundly. I glanced down at myself, still in the nightrail Drea had helped me into. I was dreaming, but I wondered if I could communicate with Todd. I went over and sat next to him, hating to wake him.

I shook his shoulder. "Todd, wake up."

He mumbled and rolled over.

I shook him harder. "Todd!"

He shot straight up. "What? Huh?" He rubbed his. "Oh, Jami, it's you. What the hell? I was having a great dream." He scratched his head and really looked at me then. "What the hell are you wearing?"

"Todd, you're still dreaming. I don't know how I am doing it, but I came into your dream during my own. I don't know how long I have, so listen up. I need you to do some things for me."

"Of course, anything you need."

"First, I need you to take the book and keep it safe. Hide it. I'll come get it sometime, but I don't know how soon. There's a lot I need to figure out and learn, and it may be a while before I am back."

"Done, what else?"

"Take care of my apartment. You have a key. Just make sure everything is okay. I'll let you know when I am here again."

"Where did you go?"

"I'm not exactly sure. Somewhere in Scotland, I think. Definitely in the past. I'll know more when I'm able to explore. I'll try to contact you again tomorrow night."

"Be careful. I know you feel this is something you have to do, but don't put yourself in danger. If it gets to be too much, just come home to me."

"Don't worry about me, Todd. I can take care of myself. But there is something here I have to do. I'm not sure what it is yet, but I can feel it in my bones. It's not time for me to return. Also, take my box as well; hide it with the book where no one can find them."

"I will. Don't worry, you can count on me." Todd went to hug me, and his arms went right through me. He sat and stared at me with a tear in his eye. "I love you."

"I love you, too. I have to go, but I'll be back. I promise."

CHAPTER 15

17th Century Scotland

In my chambers, I could tell I was still dreaming. I saw myself, Drea, and Argus lying in the bed. As I moved toward the door, Argus lifted his head and followed my movement with his eyes. He attempted to get up. "No, Argus, stay here. Guard me while I explore." He laid his head down, propping it on his front paws, and watched me leave the room.

I was able to travel outside of my body, and I took advantage of that ability. The keep had at least three levels. Stairs wound up to another floor from this one. I'd start at the bottom of the keep and work my way up.

The first floor consisted of a very large room with tables lined up along the center. I figured this must be where the meals were served. The great hall possibly; I filed a mental note to explore it later. Another smaller room had walls filled with books, large chairs, and a huge fireplace. A desk sat at one end, almost taking up an entire wall. It was the main library, most likely where the laird took care of his day to day business. Toward the rear of the keep was another room, this one a bit smaller than the library, and definitely with a more feminine air. I recognized it as where they'd taken me after I fainted outside. Then I saw Emily's sewing room. There were paintings and tapestries hung all along the hall. I wanted to take my time inspecting them, but there'd be time enough later. I made my way toward the great hall. Behind the raised dais at the far end was a doorway.

Walking through, I found the kitchen area. It consisted of two huge fireplaces with Dutch ovens above them, a long butcher-block table, and a rough sink. I found two doors behind the table; one leading to what I assumed was the pantry, and one leading outside to a rather elaborate garden. This was probably where they got their herbs and vegetables for meals. I closed both doors and turned to leave, spotting a narrow hallway. I found about a dozen doorways, all much smaller than the one to my room. I didn't open any, assuming them to be the servant's quarters, for those who didn't have families to go home to. I retraced my steps, attempting to leave, and heard a bell ringing in one of the rooms. I tried to run as the door opened.

"Don't they know it's the middle of the night? All god-fearing people should be abed," a servant grumbled as I rounded the corner to the kitchens. I stopped short, seeing one of the cooks starting the fires. I didn't know if she could see me, but I didn't want to chance it. There was nowhere close to hide. I shut my eyes and thought of my bedroom. "Bed, bed, bed," I whispered.

"Who's there?"

I became dizzy and faint. I opened my eyes to find myself in my bed chamber. With a sigh, I went to the side of the bed and stared down at my body. *Okay, Jami, now what? How do you get out of this dream?*

There was a heavy weight bearing down on me. Argus stared right into my eyes, lying on my chest and whimpering. "Hey, boy." I scratched behind his ears and the whining got louder.

"I believe he needs to go outside, but wants to make sure ye are well first," Drea said in a groggy voice from beside me.

"Oh." I smiled at Argus. "I'll be fine, boy. Go do what you need to—"

He bounded off the bed and let himself out of the room. I heard his toenails clacking down the stairs. I couldn't help but laugh. "And they thought he was dumb and useless."

"He was simply waiting for ye, I think. Our animals are smarter than we give them credit for." Drea stretched as she sat up. "Are ye hungry this morning?"

I nodded. "I'm famished, actually. If you can hand me my clothes, I'll get dressed and go with you."

She shook her head. "Emily will have my head if I allow ye to do that. She was so looking forward to speaking with ye. I will let her know ye are awake. I am sure she will bring a tray immediately."

"Can you help me get cleaned up? I want to be presentable when she comes," I inquired. "I don't have any of my toiletries here, but I know my hair needs a good brushing, as do my teeth."

"Of course."

Drea helped me take care of my morning needs then snuggled me into the bed with a mound of pillows propped behind me so I could sit up properly. "I have some things to do this morning, but I will check on ye at lunch. If ye need me before then, just send Argus to fetch me."

"Thank you, Drea, for everything." As she closed the door, Argus snuck in and jumped onto the bed, curled up, and fell right to sleep. I laughed to myself. *Just like a male, take care of himself then curl up to sleep.* Argus lifted his head and snorted at me. I laughed again as he settled in to sleep.

There was a knock at my door.

"Come in," I called out. The door opened slowly and in came a petite woman. I assumed this was Emily. I didn't remember her from last night. I waited till she spoke.

"Good morning, I am glad to see ye awake. I believe Drea mentioned I wanted to speak with ye. I am Emily O'Rourke."

"It's a pleasure to meet you," I greeted, not sure how I was suppose to act. I extended my hand.

She took mine in both of hers. "Dear, please call me Emily. I feel we will become fast friends. I had a tray prepared. Are ye hungry?" She perched on the edge of the bed.

"Yes, quite."

"Wonderful. I had the servants bring up a table and chairs as well. I thought ye might want to get out of that bed. Ye are injured, but not an invalid, as many of the men of this clan would think. What say ye? Would ye like to break yer fast by the fire?"

"That would be wonderful," I said, realizing too late I still only had on the nightrail I'd slept in.

"Fabulous." Emily stood to go over to the wardrobe. "Let me get ye a dressing gown first, before I have them bring it in." She withdrew a gorgeous emerald-green velvet dressing gown, and helped me into it. As soon as I was covered, she went to the door and instructed the servants. A parade of them brought in a small dining table, two upholstered wing-back chairs, and a tray laden with food. "Let me help ye to the chairs."

I started to hobble over and Emily placed herself under my arm, helping to guide me to the chair. I put as little weight on her as possible, afraid I might hurt her.

"I am stronger than I seem, Jami. Don't be afraid to let me help ye," she said as I sat down.

The aromas of the food hit me as I leaned forward.

"I wasn't sure what ye liked, so I had the cook prepare an array of food."

I didn't recognize everything, but there were scrambled eggs and sausages that seemed fairly innocent, so I picked those.

"There is also a pot of hot chocolate if ye like. Donovan hates that I have it brought in, but I must have my sweets." She smiled at me.

I nodded in agreement, my mouth being otherwise occupied with chewing my food.

After enjoying a fulfilling breakfast, I relaxed, stuffed to the gills. "Thank you, Emily. I feel much better."

"Ye look better. Yer color has returned to a rosy glow. How do ye feel about getting dressed and coming to sit in the gardens with me? A bit of fresh air might do ye some good."

"I would love that."

Emily went to the wardrobe again to pick out a gown for me. We were interrupted by a knock on the door. She went to answer it and let in the healer.

"I was just coming by to check up on my patient," he said. Glancing over, he saw me sitting on the edge of the bed. "Ye look much better this morning. May I inspect the wound?"

I scooted on the bed so that my leg was out straight.

"I'll need to see the back of the calf, miss."

My face burned with the heat creeping up my neck.

"Here, Jami, roll over and I'll drape the furs to keep ye warm while he looks at yer wound. I'm sure it won't take but a minute," Emily said, coming to stand by the healer, who was holding a large fur blanket.

I rolled over, trying to keep the dressing gown together and lie on my stomach.

Emily quickly placed the furs over me, leaving the injured calf available for the healer to check.

I felt a bit awkward, and I think Argus could tell I was a bit upset.

He placed himself right next to me and growled at the healer.

Emily backed away from the bed. "He's never growled before. I think he really does want to protect ye."

"I'm starting to believe that too. It's okay, Argus. He just wants to check the wound and then he'll be gone."

I held still while the healer poked and prodded around the wound, hissing as he touched it. "Well, miss, everything appears to be healing well. No infection that I can tell, and the skin is already starting to knit itself together. Ye are a lucky young woman. Nothing major was hit. Make sure to rest and don't overdo it. I will check it again tomorrow."

He instructed Emily, "Make sure this poultice is changed every four hours. It should speed up the healing and help with the pain." He left the room.

I rolled over, stared at the ceiling, and let out a breath.

"He could be an asset if any of your enemies need to be tortured," I said.

Emily laughed. "Oh, Jami, what a breath of fresh air ye are. Now let me get Drea. She can help me put this on, and we can get ye dressed and out to the gardens."

"Argus, find Drea for us. Bring her please," I told the hound.

He bounded off the bed and out the door.

"Will he really find her?" Emily asked with a bit of awe in her voice.

"He has before. I have no doubt he will this time. He's not as dumb as some here may think. He just has selective obedience." I grinned.

Emily busied herself getting everything together to put the poultice on, and then gathering what was needed to get me dressed for the journey to the garden. A few minutes later, Argus came barreling in the room with Drea on his heels.

"Ah, there ye are, Drea. I need yer help. The healer left this poultice to be put on Jami's wound and I don't think I can do it myself. Then she'd like to get dressed and go sit in the gardens with me."

They made quick work of dressing my wound and getting me changed, ready to go outside.

"It is a bit chilly today. We'll grab ye a cloak on our way out," Emily advised. They both tried to help me up, and I stopped them.

"I can get up and hobble on my own. I need to do this."

I pushed myself off the bed. As long as I didn't put too much weight on my leg, I could make it. I limped to the door. Emily and Drea followed me, and Argus stayed by my side, supporting my injured leg. I made my way down the hall, using the wall for support, but when we reached the stairs, I stopped and just stared as the steps seemed to lengthen before me.

Drea stood next to me, rubbing my arm. There were more steps than I remembered.

"Ye have a look as though ye are staring Death in the face," a male voice said from behind me.

I glanced over my shoulder to see who it was, just as Emily caught up with us. She draped a tartan over my shoulders, securing it with a clasp.

"Christan, ye arrived just in time. I believe Lady Jami may have been a little over energetic in her body's ability to heal quickly. Would ye be so kind as to assist us? I wished to take her to the rear gardens for a bit of fresh air." Emily adjusted the cloak to fall gracefully over my shoulders, encasing me in its warmth. She gave him a dazzling smile.

"Always at yer service, my lady; it would be my honor." He bowed to Emily and stepped up next to me. "Just hold on to my neck and I'll try my best not to jar yer leg." Without further discussion, he scooped me up and cradled me as though I weighed nothing.

I quickly wrapped my arms around his neck. I didn't need to add insult to injury by falling out of his big, strong arms and down the stairs.

"Jami, this is Christan. He is the head of our elite guard and Devlin's right hand man. If ye need help with anything, I am sure ye can call on him," Emily explained as we walked down the stairs and through the keep to the gardens.

"I am at yer service, Lady Jami. Call me anytime, day or night, if ye have need of my assistance." He winked as we walked out the side door of the kitchens to the gardens beyond.

I gasped as I took in my surroundings. "Oh, Emily, it's beautiful. Christan, put me down. I can walk from here."

"My lady instructed me to carry ye to the seats in the gardens, and I must do so. I cannot go against her wishes," he informed me with a smile upon his lips.

"I think you're enjoying this too much." I straightened my spine, trying to touch him as little as possible.

Christan actually laughed as he set me on my feet at the garden benches. He bowed to Emily. "If there is anything else ye need, just send for me. I must get to patrolling before Devlin has my head."

"Of course, Christan, thanks for yer assistance." Emily waved him on.

I sat on the bench and watched Christan walk away. Emily and Drea sat on either side of me. "He is kind of yummy, isn't he? Now I can sit and enjoy the view."

"Yummy?" Emily asked. "I am not sure what ye mean."

"She means he is attractive and pleasing to the eyes," Drea explained.

I laughed as they discussed my use of the word yummy. I had a feeling this would be a common occurrence. I reached down, thinking it'd be nice to have Argus out here with me, and finding his head within reach. I grinned again and patted his head, reassuring myself of his protective presence.

Devlin watched as Christan carried her to the garden benches, with Emily, Drea and that damn hound following him. He couldn't hear what they said, but she seemed to be rather friendly, holding on to Christan's neck, and allowing him to carry her. His hands gripped the railing on the balcony till his knuckles were white. Grinding his teeth, he made a mental note to speak to Christan about this. She was not to be trusted till they found out why she was truly here.

He went inside after making sure Christan had left the garden.

She laughed, and the sound sucked the breath out of him. He returned to the balcony, searching till he found them on the bench again. He couldn't take his eyes off her smiling face. She lit up the garden. It was as if all the plants leaned toward her and shivered in merriment that she laughed in their garden. The flowers seemed to be a bit brighter in color, the trees standing taller ... all for her.

He shook himself out of his reverie. His was just overreacting. Must have been the meats he'd had for breakfast. They'd tasted a bit odd. He left his chambers, and headed down to the bailey. He needed to have a discussion with Christan.

CHAPTER 16

17th Century Scotland

Emily and Drea had gone inside a while ago to take care of some things for the Festival. Though the big feast was last night, there were still people around, with games and a market place that had to be tended to. I wanted to go visit the market and see what the locals had made to sell or trade. There were also feats of strength for the men, and a hunt was planned. I opted to stay in the gardens and enjoy the sun shining down. It was so peaceful sitting there with all the plants and vegetation surrounding me. The trees made me feel safe, and it was as if the whole garden had welcomed me with open arms.

I wished, somehow, I would've been able to bring the book with me. There was so much I had yet to read, and just sitting here, I knew I needed to be doing something. I began tapping my foot, losing the peaceful feeling, and getting agitated at realizing I was basically useless here. I needed to learn more about this destiny thing. The limbs of the trees above me began to twist and shake.

I stopped tapping my foot and the limbs calmed down. *No way.* I tapped my foot again and, sure enough, the tree limbs began shaking, raining little leaves down as I increased the rhythm. *Cool.* I glanced around the garden, wondering what else I could do. My leg was feeling much better, so I decided a small walk might do me some good. I stood and took the path to the right, the one going through the flower gardens. Many of the blooms were already faded. I reached out to a foxglove and touched a blossom, imagining it the bright purple it should be when in season.

The flower perked up and the color returned.

I pulled my hand away. *Wow.* I stared at my hand, and then at the flower. *This is unreal. It's official, I have gone completely crazy.* Or maybe I hadn't; if I could travel in time, why couldn't I have magical powers?

I needed to find Drea. She might be able to help me figure out what else I could do. The letter my mother wrote said I'd come into my powers, but I had no idea what that meant. I made my way to the house, or keep, or whatever the hell they called it. It looked like a freaking castle to me. I trailed my hands along the bushes and plants as I hobbled to the door, feeling the life in each plant as I passed. It was an amazing sensation, like little zaps to my fingertips that I could feel all the way to my toes. With each one, the pain in my leg lessened. By the time I reached the door to the kitchens, my leg was almost normal, with only a slight limp in my walk. I opened the doors to mass chaos.

Servants ran around, the cook yelled out orders, pies went in the ovens, and breads came out. Two huge pots were suspended above the fires and some type of stew was cooking. My mouth watered at the smells. I made my way through as quickly as I could, trying to avoid everyone. I slipped through the doorway into the great hall. There were just a few servants cleaning. My leg started hurting a bit, so I found a chair by the fire, thinking a rest was in order. As I sat staring into the fire, a shiver ran down my spine. I scrutinized the room and saw Devlin on the stairs, gazing at me. I couldn't read his expression, so I inclined my head in greeting and gestured toward the chair next to me in invitation.

He descended the stairs and started to head my way, then he shook his head and stomped out the front door.

I couldn't help but laugh, I honestly thought he was afraid of me. The door opened again. Expecting Devlin to have returned, I watched the entry way, only to see Drea walking toward me. I was happy to see her.

She sat in the chair next to me. "Do not let Emily see ye here. She will have a fit if she knew ye walked in by yerself." She grinned at me. "How is yer leg feeling?"

"It was feeling almost normal outside, but by the time I walked through the kitchens and in here it started to hurt again, so I sat here to give it a rest." I debated whether to tell her about what I experienced in the gardens, and decided to wait till we were somewhere a bit more private.

"Makes sense." Drea nodded. "The gardens seemed to have a calming effect on ye. I could feel the power surrounding ye while we sat there."

"I can't explain it, but I think you're right."

"So, what would ye like to do today?"

"I would love to visit the market."

"That is quite a bit of walking. I'm not sure if Emily or the healer would approve." Drea frowned.

"I'll take it easy. If we could find a walking stick or cane, it'd help take the weight and pressure off my leg. I'll take care and rest when I need to. Please, Drea, I need to get out. I feel stifled in here, like I can't breathe."

"Very well, I will go find a sturdy walking stick. Ye stay right here till I get back."

I nodded and reclined in my chair. Drea left. I gazed into the fire and started to feel a constriction in my chest, my breathing becoming heavy. I couldn't pull my eyes away. The flames formed a face, its mouth moving, trying to talk, but I couldn't hear any words. I started to panic and was about to jump out of my chair, when someone sat next to me.

"Here ye are. I didn't see ye in the gardens when I went to assist ye inside," Christan said, sitting next to me.

"I'm not an invalid, just injured. I made my way just fine, thank you very much," I huffed. I gazed into the fire, but the face was gone. I filed that away to speak to Drea about as well. I turned to find Christan staring at me.

"Is everything all right, Lady Jami?" he asked. "Ye look a bit pale."

"Yes, everything's fine. I'm just waiting on Drea so we can go walk in the market."

The front door slammed.

I assumed it'd be Drea returning, but Devlin barreled down on us instead.

"So, this is where I find ye, shirking yer duties, Christan."

"And good morrow to ye, Devlin," Christan replied as he stood. "I am simply checking on Lady Jami, per Emily's request."

"Ye have more important duties to attend to than to be Emily's errand boy." Devlin came up behind us, crossing his arms and looming over me. "I need ye to assign the patrols for the day."

"The men already have their orders, and the first watch set out a good thirty minutes ago. I had a short break and, seeing Emily had her hands full with the child, I offered to check on Lady Jami for her," Christan informed Devlin. "I see she is fine and in good hands with Drea, so I will head out to the lists and get the rest of the men started on their daily training." Christan bowed to Devlin, and then to me. "Till we meet again, Lady Jami. I hope ye enjoy yer stroll in the market."

"Thank you, Christan." I beamed at him.

He spun to leave, and Devlin stared him down as he passed.

I couldn't help but admire Devlin's physique as he stood there. Muscles rippling under his skin as his arms tensed for just a minute when Christan passed. Devlin returned his gaze to me with a scowl on his face. "I thought the healer said ye were to rest yer leg? I don't see how gallivanting about the keep is resting," Devlin growled.

"I thank you for your concern, but I know my own limitations, Lord Devlin. I promise you if I feel fatigued at all, I will return to my room."

"Damn women," he harrumphed as he walked away.

My mouth went dry and my heart sped. I saw the definition in his shoulders and legs as he walked, the muscles moving beneath the skin in a sensuous dance. I was already imagining him naked, and what those muscles would feel like beneath my hands, my tongue.

Shaking myself out of my trance, I dropped my eyes to the fire as heat crept up my neck. What the hell was I thinking imagining him naked? Oh, my god, my hormones were running wild.

"Jami, I found the perfect thing," Drea said as she walked in.

I glanced up to see she'd brought me a gorgeous walking stick. It was carved out of a thick piece of wood, though I couldn't tell what type. As she brought it closer, I saw little fairies had been carved all along the length of it, and the top was shaped in an octagon. I just knew it would fit my hand perfectly.

I took it from her. "Drea, it's beautiful. Where on earth did you find it?"

She beamed as she sat down. "My father made it. He met me outside and said he saw ye would need it. He had started working on it before we even arrived, and made it especially for ye."

"Oh, Drea, I can't accept this. He obviously put a lot of time and effort into it. I just thought you would find a sturdy stick or something." I shook my head as I tried to hand it to her.

"Nonsense, Jami. It's a gift to ye. Father fashioned it out of the trunk of a young Rowan tree. It will aid ye when ye need it, and will help ye to connect to the nature around ye. Please take it. It would make my father very happy."

How could I refuse after everything he put into it? "Thank him for me. I'm honored and will cherish it always."

"Ye can thank him yerself. He has a stall set up in the market. Shall we go?" She extended her hand to me.

I took it and, with the help of the walking stick, stood. I tested the stick out and found it could hold my weight easily. "Let's do this." I giggled. "I can't believe how excited I am to get outside."

"It's no surprise." Drea laughed. "It's the fairy blood talking to ye. Remember to stay open to it. Trust yer instincts and if anything scares ye, talk to me."

"I will," I said, and we ventured out of the keep.

It was beautiful outside. I smelled the earth as we walked down the steps. We hit the ground and, at the first tap of the walking stick, I felt it vibrate. I slowed to examine the sensation. It wasn't like the humming of my cuff, but more of a rhythm vibration. I played around as we walked, placing the end of the stick on solid ground, in patches of grass, among wildflowers. Each time the vibration was different. Everything had its own rhythm. My heart became lighter the more we walked.

I perused each stall. Many of the villagers had come to peddle their wares. There were furs of all kinds, spun wool, tartan fabrics, handmade jams and jellies, smoked meat, pastries, bolts of fabric, ribbon, and much more. We arrived at her father's stall. He had all kinds of little wooden toys, walking sticks, buttons ... just about anything that could be carved from wood. I noticed a box. It was exactly like the one I had at home. I lovingly ran my hand over the top. It sang to me and tears sprang to my eyes. It was just large enough for my book to be able to fit in it. I wanted to ask how much it cost, but realized I had no money. I walked away, saddened for some reason.

"It speaks to ye, doesn't it?" Drea's father asked.

"Yes," I answered him.

"Jami, this is my father, Alexandrou. Father, this is Jami O'Malley."

It was actually Jami Morgan, but I didn't correct her.

"It's a pleasure to meet you." I extended my hand.

Alexandrou took it between his and closed his eyes, grasping my hand briefly, and then releasing it. "Yes, they all sing to ye, don't they? In their own ways, but that one more than the others. Ye have much potential inside ye. Ye must open yerself up to receive it." He walked over to the box and returned with it in his hands. "It is yers. It will be the only way ye can bring yer beloved book with ye. Place this next to yer bed on the night stand and, when ye next visit yer home, it will be with ye. Place yer book inside and ye will find it there when ye awaken," he instructed me.

I took the box from him, smiling in thanks.

"But be careful, my child, too much dream walking and ye might not find yer way home." He pulled my head down and kissed my forehead. "May the blessing of light be on ye. Light without and light within. May the blessed sunlight shine on ye and warm yer heart till it glows like a great peat fire."

I became suddenly weak. "I think it's time I return to my room.

I'm tired and a bit hungry."

"Of course. Can ye make the journey, or shall I find someone to help?" she asked with a concerned note to her voice.

I hated to admit it, but I was pretty sure I couldn't walk that far on my own. "I think you'll have to find someone to help me. I'm not sure I can stand much longer."

Drea's father brought a stool over to me. "Sit child, wait here while Drea fetches help." He said to Drea, "Hurry child, she needs her rest, and quickly."

Drea took off to find assistance, and I wobbled on the stool, trying to keep myself awake. I didn't want to humiliate myself by falling off the stool. I don't know how long I sat there, listening to one of the musicians play a lonely tune on his fiddle, before Drea returned with help in tow.

Christan was staring down at me.

"Did someone wear herself out?" He smirked.

"I guess I pushed it a little too much. I hate to ask for your help, but I'm not sure I can make it on my own," I admitted grudgingly.

"It's my pleasure to help a fair maiden in distress," he joked. He leaned down and placed one arm behind my back and one under my knees, taking care not to touch or jar my injured leg. "Now, like the last time, just hang onto my neck and I'll have ye in yer chambers in no time."

My arms encircled his neck. I glanced over his shoulder at Drea. "Can you please bring my things, Drea, before you grab us some food?"

"Of course, Jami, I'll be right behind ye," she assured me.

Christan started toward the keep and I was so tired I could barely hold my head up. I was trying, but not very well.

"Ye can lay yer head on my shoulder, my lady. I won't bite, promise," he said with a wink.

I was too tired to even retort. I simply laid my head down and heaved a sigh. About half way to the keep, Devlin barged toward us. "What do ye think ye are doing, Christan?"

I cringed at the sound of his voice. He was starting to piss me off, always barging in when he wasn't needed, barking orders and yelling. "He's assisting me to my chambers, if you must know. I didn't realize how far we had walked and I couldn't make it by myself. I sent Drea to fetch him to help. Now if you don't mind, kindly let us pass so I can go lie down," I snapped at him.

Christan twisted his head away to hide a smile.

Devlin stepped closer, "Christan, I need ye to guard the gates this afternoon so Bran can give the young pups a workout in the lists. I'll help Lady Jami from here." He placed his arms just behind Christan's on my back and behind my knees.

"It won't take but a minute for Christan to take me the rest of the way, Lord Devlin. I'm sure you can do without him for that short time period." I snorted.

"No, he is needed elsewhere. I cannot spare him at this moment." He pulled me to him, jerking my arms from around Christan's neck.

I crossed my arms and glared up at him. He nodded to Christan. "Off with ye. I'll see ye before evening meal." Devlin turned toward the keep, taking big strides, so much so that Drea had to jog to keep up with us. I peeked over Devlin's shoulder to see Christan turning toward the gate, shaking his head with a smile on his face.

"You know, you're an ass," I told Devlin, and clapped my hand over my mouth. I couldn't believe I'd said that out loud.

"Aye, I've been called worse, lass. Ye can't be taking my guards whenever ye need help. They have a job to do, and it's not catering to yer every whim." He tightened his grip around me.

My body heated in reaction to being so close to him. I didn't want it to, but I had no control over myself. I leaned into his chest and almost molded my body to his, as much as I could at this awkward angle. He smelled of wood smoke, pine, and something completely earthly and male. I inhaled deeply at his neck.

Devlin froze at the bottom of the steps to the keep. He gazed down at me with hooded eyes, and what I saw there both scared and excited me. We were so close; all I had to do was stretch up and I could kiss those luscious lips. They were so full, and just asking to be nibbled on.

Drea passed us. "This way, Lord Devlin."

He broke our eye contact, then took the stairs two at a time, taking care not to jostle me.

I laid my head against his chest, nuzzled under his chin. This was right and, when he carried me over the threshold of the keep, a jolt went through me. I think he sensed it too, as his steps faltered just a bit before he caught himself and continued up to my chamber. He set me on the bed and quickly retreated to the doorway. "If ye need anything else, please let Emily or the servants know." He gazed at me one more time, while tightening his fists, then pivoted and left.

I lay down with a sigh.

Drea regarded me with one brow cocked.

"Don't ask, Drea. I don't even know." I didn't want to feel this attraction; Devlin was an ass, or arse as they say here. A royal donkey's arse, but I couldn't deny my reaction to him. It was all so confusing.

Drea went to the door and called to a servant down the hall. She instructed the maid to gather a lunch tray for us, then stepped inside. As she was closing the door, Argus bounded through and up onto the bed with me.

"There you are. Where were you about fifteen minutes ago when the ogre showed up to carry me? I could have used a bit of the protective spirit then." I reached down to pet him and touched flowers in his fur. I stopped to take a good long look at him, and burst out laughing. He had wildflowers woven all through his fur, and I could swear he had a smile on his face. "Ahh, I see you have found a younger mistress to play with, eh?" He woofed, and snuggled up beside me, nudging my hand with his nose, and licking my palm as I raised it to pet him again. "I forgive you, boy, and I don't blame you at all. I would stay out of his way too if I could."

I was so tired. I closed my eyes, intending only to rest till the food came, but fell immediately into a deep sleep.

CHAPTER 17

Current Day

I must have been thinking of Todd and my book as I went to sleep, because when I opened my eyes, I found myself in my apartment, watching Todd sitting in my reading chair and paging through my book.

"Hi, Todd."

He jumped out of the chair, startled. "Oh, my god, Jami! You scared the daylights out of me." He rushed over to hug me, but I stopped him before he reached me, not sure if I'd be able to touch him. This was different than the last time I'd visited in a dream. I didn't feel quite so whole.

"What's been going on? Is everything okay?"

"Yeah, I mean your mom is bugging me about where you are and why you just up and left, but as long as I ignore the calls, everything is okay. I was worried I wouldn't see you again. I have been trying to get this book to show me what it showed you, thinking maybe if you were in trouble, it would let me know," he said sheepishly.

"Oh, Todd. No, I am fine, but there is so much I have to do. I came to check on you and to get my book. I need it with me. I miss you so much, but when I'm there, I feel like I'm home. I've never felt this way. The only thing missing is you."

"Take me with you. It's no fun being here, day to day without you. It's just not the same. I don't have anyone to wine and whine with, no one to drool on the new season's designer shoes, no one to plan a dream trip to Scotland with." I saw tears starting in his eyes. "Jami, I need to know, are you coming home for good?"

"I can't answer that right now."

Todd turned away to stare out the window. "No matter how much I miss you, I only want the best for you. I want you to be happy, and

I know you weren't here. So if staying there, with all those big, hulking, dreamy Scottish men is best for you, then you stay."

"Aww, are you jealous?" I laughed.

He whirled around with a big grin on his face. "Damn straight I'm jealous."

I noticed the box Drea's father had given me on the table in front of my reading chair. "Todd, I need you to put the book in that box for me."

Todd placed the book gently inside. When he closed the lid, the box faded out. He spun around, eyes wide. "Wow, if I hadn't seen that with my own eyes, I wouldn't believe it. Oh, and speaking of boxes, I've been carrying this around with me, waiting for you to return. Something strange happened after you left last time."

Todd pulled my jewel box out of his messenger bag and set it down on the table. I went to it and noticed words had been engraved below the design on the top. I gazed at Todd for an answer. He shrugged. "When I got up that morning I took a shower and came out to pack your things up to take with me, and it was there. The words just appeared. I don't know what they say, but I'm sure they're important, so I wanted to make sure you saw them."

I stared down at the case again and realized this was the same language I'd been reading. The words read, "Go home."

I tilted my head, thinking to myself. I touched them. *"Go home."*

Just like the box with my book, this one faded and disappeared. I contemplated Todd. "I guess that means they'll be waiting for me at home."

Todd nodded at me. I watched a tear escape down his face. He straightened to his full height. "Don't you worry about me. I'll hold down the fort here. Just let me know how things turn out. I have to have something to dangle in front of your mother." He winked at me.

I took a step back. He resembled Christan in that moment. "Todd, didn't you say at one point you have Scottish in your family?"

"You know that. It's one of the reasons we always planned to travel to Scotland." He smirked.

I smiled lovingly. "You know what, I'm going to be just fine. And so will you. I'll find a way to let you know it." I scanned all the things in my apartment, all the things I loved about it: my reading chair, my bookshelves, the nook to the kitchen, and all my pictures of Scotland. I walked up to Todd.

"All of this is yours now so take care of things and watch out for yourself. I'll try to visit again, but it may only be in your dreams. Remember I love you and, if it hadn't been for you and your support, I wouldn't have found my destiny."

I sniffed, realizing I was crying. I began wavering. "I have to go, Todd. Remember me, take our memories, and keep them with you." I walked over and brushed a kiss across his cheek.

As I gazed out the window one last time, he whispered, "I'll never forget you, Jami. I've always loved you."

17th Century Scotland

"Jami, wake up. Dear, it's time to wake up." Drea lightly shook me. "Come on, Jami. We need to change the bandage on yer leg."

I opened my eyes to see Drea sitting next to me on the bed, and a small tray on the nightstand with fresh bandages and more of the poultice cream.

I pulled up to a sitting position, stretching and rubbing the sleep from my eyes. "How long have I been asleep?"

"About three hours. I hate to wake ye, but the healer says we need to change the bandages and ye need to get some food in ye."

"Fine."

Drea picked up the tray as I moved the covers and rolled over so she could get to the wound on my leg. She untied the bandage and removed it, then took a damp cloth to clean off the poultice. I heard her sharp intake of breath.

I peered over my shoulder. "What is it? Is it worse?"

"No, I can't believe my eyes. It's almost healed. There is just a bright pink scar." She stared up at me. "How does it feel?"

I flexed my foot tentatively, just a slight twinge, but no pain. "It feels fine, doesn't hurt at all."

Drea moved the tray and stood. "Try walking."

I rolled over and scooted off the bed. I stood slowly, putting weight on the leg. Still no pain. Then I put all my weight on my leg and no pain. I walked around the room a bit and not even a limp. I scrunched my eyebrows at Drea. "How?"

She shook her head. "I don't know, it's a blessing. Maybe fast healing is part of yer powers. I am not questioning it, nor should ye. Just be happy with this; ye won't be confined to certain areas." She beamed. "Let's get something to eat."

I nodded in agreement. "Let's. I'm starved." My stomach growled at the same time and I laughed.

Drea set the tray down on the table by the fire.

I snapped my fingers for Argus. He lopped off the bed to stand at my side. "Shall we go in search of food, boy?" I scratched behind his ears.

I followed Drea out and down the stairs. It was so good not having to depend on someone else to get me around the keep. We took our time. I asked Drea about the pictures and tapestries we came across, and she told me as much as she could about them. "I don't know much about the family history here. We should find Emily. She could give ye more information than I."

"I don't want to bother her now. What you're telling me is a good start." I grinned. I couldn't help myself; the home spoke to me. The wood used for the railing was warm under my hands. I sensed all the hands that had rubbed against it through the years. It was as if the keep was happy to see me up and about. I giggled to myself as we walked into the great hall. The rushes on the floor had been replaced that morning, and I smelled the heather woven into them to help keep a fresh scent wafting up to us as we walked. The scent tickled my nose and made me happy.

"Lady Jami, should ye be out of bed? We don't want ye stressing yerself too much," Christan asked, smiling at me.

"I appreciate your concern, but I'm much better. Practically healed, watch." I walked and did a model turn. "See? No limp and no pain." I smirked.

"In that case, may I escort ye lovely ladies to a table near the kitchens?" He extended an elbow to each of us.

"Why thank you, sir." I curtsied and took his arm.

Drea took his other elbow, and the three of us walked the rest of the way.

I was grinning and enjoying myself. We arrived at the tables and Christan assisted each of us into our chairs. "I hate to leave ye ladies, but duty calls." With a bow and a wink, he walked out.

I peeked over at Drea and couldn't contain my giggle. After she'd instructed a servant to fetch us a tray of meats and cheeses and a pitcher of cider, I focused on Emily barreling down on our table. "What are ye doing out of bed? The kitchen could have sent the tray to yer room," she huffed.

"Emily, I'm fine. Truly, my leg is almost healed." I placed my hand on her arm. "Please don't get upset. We didn't tell you right away because we didn't want to interrupt what you may have been doing. Please, forgive me."

She gazed down at me, then plopped into the chair next to me. Taking my hand in hers, she swiveled. "Truly, but how? The healer thought it would take weeks to heal. I don't understand."

"We don't really know, either. Drea thinks it may have something to do with the fairy blood in me, and the gifts it brings. I'm not going to question it right now. I'm just happy I can walk on my own again, and to have things back to normal. Or as normal as possible."

"Very well." Emily nodded and let go of my hand. "Then let us eat, and after; Drea and I will give ye a full tour of the keep and its grounds."

"That would be wonderful," I agreed. The servants brought our food and drink and we dug in ... or at least I did. I acted like a pig at the trough compared to Emily. She took such dainty bites, and with such poise. Here I shoveled food in my mouth as if I hadn't eaten in weeks. But honestly, that's what it seemed like. I realized when I traveled in my sleep that it took a lot out of me. I needed to refuel if I would be exploring before evening meal.

"Oh, Jami, I have a surprise for ye, and since ye will be able to make it down for evening meal with us, I shall share it with ye when we return from our tour." Emily bubbled with excitement.

I couldn't do anything but nod, my mouth being otherwise occupied with food. I quickly washed my food down with a mug of cider, and the three of us headed out. Emily showed me everything. We started outside with the courtyard. She showed me the stables, the milling room, the spinning rooms, the ale rooms—I was amazed that they made their own ale—and finally the guard house. We were stopped many times on our tour by the villagers, children, or just people passing by. Emily took the time to introduce me to each one, we chatted with them all. I saw their people loved and adored her, and she returned the feeling.

We made our way around the bailey. Emily pointed out what they called the barracks, and she explained that was where the warriors were housed. Those without families, or those just starting their training. They were provided a place to sleep, meals, clothing, and a small stipend for their service. Then we went on around to the gardens, which I'd seen already, and out a door in the rear of the wall. Emily took us up to the lists to watch some of the training. We heard the ring of metal on metal before we reached the field. As we walked up to the waist-high rock wall lining one edge of the fields, the hairs on my neck stood on end and my breathing got heavier. I stared ahead, seeing Devlin shirtless and taking one of what I assumed to be the newer recruits through a series of training exercises.

His skin glowed with the sheen of sweat. His hair was held off his face at the nape of his neck with a tie of some sort. His muscles flowed like water under his skin with each swing of the broadsword. My mouth was dry, and I couldn't take my eyes off him. Everything faded away, and it was just Devlin and I in that field. My fingers itched to trace his rippling muscles, and my lips wanted to taste every drop of sweat on his body. A throbbing began in my core, and radiated out to the rest of my body.

"If ye keep staring at him like that, ye are going to burn a hole in his back," Christan whispered in my ear.

I quickly averted my gaze, heat creeping up my neck, my breathing still ragged, and my body singing and straining to reach Devlin. I took a few deep breaths before I could look at Christan. When I brought myself to meet his eyes, he simply winked at me and walked on.

It was very quiet in the lists, and the hairs on my neck were at attention again. I swung around to see Devlin staring straight at me. We locked eyes and he came striding over. His legs ate up the distance in no time.

He nodded at Drea and Emily in greeting, then stopped right in front of me. My eyes met the muscles in his chest. "I thought ye were resting in yer chambers, not traipsing around and wearing yerself out again."

My eyes trailed up over his chest, noticing the tendons in his neck were strained, and seeing droplets of sweat. I followed their path up to his chin, taking in his supple lips, his nose that had a slight bump in it, as though it'd been broken in youth, and finally landing on his eyes. What I saw there stopped my breath. Anger, curiosity, and passion all swirled around in their depths.

I opened and closed my mouth several times, but no sound came out.

"Lord Devlin, her leg is much better, practically healed. We don't know how, but it seems to be a miracle," Drea said.

Devlin glanced at her, then at me again, and quirked an eyebrow. "Is that so?"

I nodded, feeling like an idiot, still unable to bring myself to talk. My legs were starting to go weak and the throbbing in my core was unbearable. I found myself leaning toward him, breathing in his scent: woods, earth, and sweaty male. An intoxicating combination.

If I didn't stop I'd make a fool of myself right here in front of all his warriors, but I didn't care. I wanted to taste him so bad.

He grabbed ahold of my upper arms and leaned down. "Who are ye?" he whispered. His lips so close all I had to do was lean up to kiss him. "Stop this before ye make a fool out of both of us."

He set me on my heels and the trance was broken.

It was as if a bucket of ice-cold water had been poured over my head. I gazed around, only to find everyone watching us. "Lord Devlin, my apologies. It was not my intent to make a fool out of you. Your lovely sister-in-law was simply giving me a tour of the keep and its grounds. I won't take any more of your time." I glanced toward Emily, and then at Devlin. "If you'll excuse us, we'll be on our way."

I stepped away and Emily came up to take my arm.

"We shall see ye at evening meal, Devlin. Please make sure to wash up before ye join us at the table," Emily said with a bit of haughtiness to her tone. She twirled me and started off toward the cliffs, which were the next stop on the tour.

Drea caught up with us, and both women flanked me as we made our way to the cliff.

The breeze became cooler as we got closer to the edge. Emily stopped us about a hundred yards from the edge. I tried to continue on, but she held fast to my arm. "It's not safe to get any closer than this; the rocks are unstable."

I glanced through Emily, to Drea. "I need to get closer."

I knelt down and placed my hands on the ground, asking with my heart if it was safe. The rocks answered me, warming and humming, assuring me I'd be safe. I stood and gently removed Emily's hand from my arm. "I'll be fine; it's safe."

Emily started to protest.

"Emily, let her go. She would never put herself in danger. This land will do her no harm," Drea said.

Emily, a worried crease to her brow, gave a quick nod.

I continued to the edge, the air thickening, weighted down by the mist floating up from the rocks below. I raised my head, closed my eyes, and accepted the gift of the land and the sea. The waves crashed against the rocks below, sending more salt spray into the air. I slowly raised my arms, with a genuine smile emerging on my face. I heard the rocks sing to me through the soles of my shoes. My body swayed to the vibrations.

Drea moved up behind me and my smile widened. "I'm home, Drea, the land and the sea call to me." The music of the waves hitting the rocks fell into tune with the beats of my heart. I opened my hands fully to the sky, giving thanks and sharing my happiness with the elements around me.

Drea gasped behind me. Opening my eyes, I saw the waves had increased in height, almost as if trying to meet my hands in the sky. I was giddy. My body was alive with power. It was radiating off me. The intensity of the waves grew. "Jami, ye need to calm the sea." She scanned all around. "Ye need to release the sea, let it return home."

"How?" My body hummed and I wasn't sure how to stop it.

"Close yer eyes, calm yer heart, and release it," Drea instructed.

With my eyes closed, I took a deep, calming breath and lowered my arms. As they met my sides, I instinctively rotated my palms toward the sea and sent out a prayer of thanks, as well as a promise to come and play again. I relaxed as the energy left me through my palms.

"Jami," Drea gasped.

I opened my eyes to a rainbow forming from the rock ledge and extending out to the sea. I twisted my head to Drea, and found a mask of peace and happiness upon her face.

"Ye did that, Jami. We need to go talk to my father. He may be able to help ye harness and control yer powers."

I nodded and joined Emily again. She'd gone completely white. I rushed over, afraid she might faint. "Emily, are you alright?"

She gazed at my hands, then at my face in concerned awe. "Did ye do that, Jami?"

I could only nod. I was afraid of what I saw on her face. Would she think me some kind of witch now? Would she run away and hide? Or worse yet, would she ask me to leave? I stood there waiting, fear sitting cold in my belly.

"That was amazing. I don't know how to put my feelings into words. I was scared watching ye walk out to the ledge, worried ye might fall. But then when ye raised yer arms, it was like a sense of peace washed over me. Ye did that, Jami. Ye calmed me. And the joy I saw on yer face. I don't know; ye were meant to be here. I have seen ye here before." She gazed into my eyes and I saw tears forming there. She wrapped her arms around me in a fierce hug. "Thank ye."

I hugged her, if a bit awkwardly. I didn't understand what she meant, but I needed to comfort her.

"Let's head toward the keep," Drea suggested. "It's almost time to get ready for evening meal."

Emily stepped away. "Yes, let's. I have a surprise for ye, Jami, and I think ye'll like it." She grinned like a little school girl with a secret, took my arm, and lead us to the keep.

CHAPTER 18

17ᵗʰ Century Scotland

Devlin stood at the edge of the lists, watching the three women walk toward the keep. He didn't know what he'd just witnessed, but something called to him deep inside every time he laid eyes on Jami. He wasn't happy about it. He didn't have time for frivolous women. He left that to his younger brother, Darrick. Devlin enjoyed the flesh of a woman, but only when his needs demanded it.

It'd taken all the control he had not to go running to Jami when she raised her arms at the edge of the cliff. She'd stood too damn close for his liking. She could have fallen off, the dumb woman. Those rocks weren't stable. One false move or a foot in the wrong place and she could have gone over the edge. Just the thought of it stole his breath away and constricted his heart. As he'd watched her, his body screamed at him to go to her, to pull her from the ledge, and crush her to him. His body yearned to be close to her. His need to be inside her was almost uncontrollable.

He scowled at the road his thoughts took. Dammit, this woman meant nothing to him. She was just some lost girl his sister-in-law had taken in. She meant nothing to him, though his heart tried to tell him differently.

"What's put that sour expression on yer face?" Christan asked, when he brought Devlin his jerkin and belt.

"Nothing, I was just thinking of the training half of these new men need." He pulled his jerkin over his head and buckled his belt, then sheathed his broadsword.

"I think they all have great potential, and have come great lengths in the short time we have worked with them."

"Yes, but we need more men trained and ready now. I have a feeling this lull won't last. The Mulligans are planning something; I can feel it in my bones, and we need to have the men patrolling more often." Devlin shook his head. "Our army is low on men as it is, and the increase in patrols will thin us out even more. We need to get the new recruits trained faster so they can help out." Devlin headed toward the keep walls.

"I understand, Devlin. A couple more weeks and we'll have a fresh round of men ready to take on that responsibility."

"I am afraid we won't have a couple of weeks. We may not even have a couple of days."

"What do ye know that ye aren't telling me?" Christan stopped him with a hand on his shoulder.

Devlin faced him. "The gypsy's father came to me last night and told me of a vision he had. A war unlike any we've seen is on the horizon. We have to be prepared, he said. The Mulligans have enlisted help this time, but he couldn't see who or what."

"Och, ye don't believe in that nonsense, remember?" Christan laughed.

Devlin looked up. "I do now. This time he showed me. I can't explain it, but he showed me the vision, Christan, and it's not good." Devlin continued inside the keep walls.

I found a bath ready for me when we returned to my chambers. Emily had gone to freshen up and change after we entered the keep. Drea had also gone to her chambers, but reassured me she'd come assist me after my bath. I walked in to find a huge copper tub filled with steaming water, and a small table set beside it with bath oils for me to choose from. Argus snoozed on the bed. He lifted his head as I walked in, then promptly went to sleep.

I pulled the stopper on several bottles before deciding on a soft lilac scent. I liberally poured it into the water. The aroma wafted up and tickled my nose. I removed my over dress, and the linen shift and tights. I was down to my bra and underwear before I realized they were the only set I had. I removed them and set them aside. I'd have to wash them by hand, and hope they dried in time to get dressed for evening meal.

I sank down into the water with a sigh of pleasure. I was a bit grimy after two days of sponge baths. I laid my head against the tub and let the water soothe me. I submerged myself once to wet my hair, then sat back up to look for something to scrub the dirt off with. I found a linen wash cloth on the table and began to wash. I was almost done when I heard a knock at the door.

Argus leapt off the bed and loped toward the door, his tail wagging.

"Who is it?" I called out.

"Drea"

"Come in."

Argus greeted her with doggy kisses and walked over to the tub with her. He sat between the two of us.

"I thought ye might need some help rinsing yer hair."

"I haven't even gotten to my hair yet. I was just enjoying the fact I had a warm bath in my room." I sighed.

"Then let me." Drea picked up the soap and lathered my hair, gently combing the soap through to make sure each strand was clean. She took the pitcher and instructed me to sit forward. She rinsed my hair, then grabbed the towels hanging by the fire. "We need to get ye dried off and dressed; evening meal will be soon."

I took one of the towels and wrapped myself as I stood in the tub. I stepped out onto another she'd laid on the floor and went to sit in the chair in front of the fire.

Drea dried my hair with the towel she had in her hands. "Yer hair won't be dry in time, but I could plait it for ye so that it will be out of the way."

"Thank you. That would be great," I said as another knock sounded at my door.

Argus didn't even budge this time.

Drea went to see who it was.

Emily walked in. "Oh my, we need to get ye dressed. They will be expecting us soon." She skipped over to the wardrobe as Drea came to fix my hair. Emily opened the doors and giggled. "Surprise!"

The wardrobe was full of clothes. Everything from daily overdresses to elaborate velvet gowns.

"Emily, how did you do this?" I asked. I wanted to get up and go see them all, but Drea pulled on my hair as I attempted to stand. I sat still, waiting for her to finish.

"Oh, it was nothing. My sewing ladies had so much fun putting these together. I think the green velvet would do nicely for supper tonight."

"I agree." Drea nodded. "There, all done." She released my hair and I went to the wardrobe. The fabrics were so soft, and the stitch work was amazing.

Emily pulled out the dress she'd indicated and the band on my arm hummed. She then pulled out a few undergarments from the trunk at the end of the bed. "All right, let's get ye dressed."

I gazed longingly at my bra and underwear. I couldn't put them on. With a sigh, I walked to the bed and picked up the first thing Emily set out for me: a long camisole. I slipped it over my head and tied the lacing on the front to keep it closed. The stockings came next. These were only thigh high, but had a ribbon on them to help keep them up. Then came the corset. Emily helped lace it, so it wouldn't be too tight, but still held everything where it was supposed to be. Last came the dress.

Drea helped me get it over my head.

She settled it and showed me how to tie it down the underside of my arm on each side. This helped tighten the bodice and give it the womanly shape Emily's had. The sleeves were full length with a slit open from the shoulder to wrist along the outside of the arm. The bust was cut low enough to show just a bit of cleavage.

Emily ran to the door and spoke to someone outside. The next thing I knew, I was staring at myself in her full-length mirror. My jaw dropped. I didn't recognize myself; I had a glow about me as I spun this way and that to see the whole dress. It was gorgeous. I loved it. I gave Emily a big hug. "Thank you, Emily. I feel at home, and that hasn't happened in a long while."

I spun again and noticed my arm cuff winking at me out the slit in my sleeve.

"Oh, stop. Ye'r welcome. I enjoyed doing it. Now, if we are ready, we should head down. I am sure the men are waiting on us." She took my arm.

Argus followed us out of the room and down the stairs. He stayed by my side as we entered the great hall to find most of the clan was already sitting and preparing for the meal.

Emily walked me up to one of the tables next to the dais, where she and her husband would sit. Drea sat a couple of tables away with her father and sisters. There was an empty seat next to Christan.

He stood and pulled out the chair for me.

I gazed up at Christan, and then to Emily, who inclined her head to Christan and let my arm go. "We will talk after the meal," she whispered and continued her way to her seat.

I sat as gracefully as possible, and smiled at Christan as he pushed my chair in.

"Thank you."

"Ye are most welcome, my lady, and may I say ye are very lovely tonight." He sat next to me. "I am honored to sit next to ye. Though I warn ye, Devlin may blow his top when he sees that mutt lying at yer feet."

"Well then, Lord Devlin will just have to deal with it, won't he? Argus won't be a problem, of that I can promise, unless anyone has ill wishes toward me."

Argus growled in agreement.

Christan laughed as Devlin walked into the great hall. He stopped short when he saw Jami sitting next to his best friend. She was smiling up at him, and she was stunning. He'd never seen her in anything but the normal day wear of the clan. His blood stirred at the sight of her, his heartbeat sped up, and his pants became a bit tight and uncomfortable.

He normally sat across the table from Christan, but he wouldn't make it through this meal if he sat there tonight. He searched around the great hall, looking for another seat, but none were to be found. He continued his way to the table, dreading the hour ahead.

"There ye are, friend. I was beginning to wonder if ye were going to grace us with yer presence," Christan greeted.

Devlin sat down with a plop and Argus growled. "What the hell is that mutt doing at the table?"

Jami bristled at his tone. "Argus is hurting no one. I see no reason why he can't lie at my feet."

"The meal table is no place for a dog, especially one as useless as that one."

Argus growled again.

Jami placed her hand along his fur to settle him. "He's not useless. Actually he's rather intelligent. He was just waiting for the right person to choose as his master. I can see why. There don't seem to be many humans around who can match his intelligence."

Oh. My. God. Where had that come from? I immediately realized I'd just insulted one of the lords of the keep and heat rose into my face.

Argus licked my hand, settling down on his paws.

Christan busted out laughing as the servants brought in the evening meal. "We have a feisty one here, don't we, Devlin?" He winked at me.

Devlin simply glared across the table.

He had my skin tingling. That warm feeling started in my core again, and slowly spiraled out to every nerve in me. My body was on fire under his glare, but I couldn't look away. I wouldn't have him seeing me as some weak woman he could boss around as he saw fit. The longer he stared, the warmer I got. My breasts became heavy and ached with the need to be touched. I found myself leaning toward him, and stopped just before I fell into my plate. It was then that Devlin looked away and I could finally focus on my food, but I was no longer hungry. Another hunger had been ignited, and it had nothing to do with food.

I picked at my plate, pushing my food around, and forcing myself to take a few bites. My blood hummed in my veins, and I envisioned Devlin and I, naked atop the furs of my bed, in front of the fire, entwined with one another. I glanced over to find Devlin staring at me with smoldering eyes. My mouth went dry and I grabbed my goblet to quench my thirst. The wine didn't seem to help. It only fueled the fire in my belly. I needed to get out of there before I made a complete fool of myself. I excused myself from the table.

Argus followed.

I found Drea's table.

"Drea, I am not feeling well. I am going up early to lie down."

"Jami, are ye alright; would ye like me to come with ye?"

"Yes, I will be fine. Just a bit of a headache; can you let Emily know where I have gone?"

"Of course, and I will come check on ye when I am finished"

I nodded and left the great hall. As soon as I was away from Devlin, my body started to cool. Instead of heading up the stairs, I went out the front door to the courtyard. It began to drizzle and I raised my face to the sky, letting the rain cool my skin and wash away the heat in my cheeks.

Argus took off to run with the other hounds outside. I couldn't help but smile to myself. To be that carefree would be wonderful.

"Ye are getting soaked out here."

I smelled damp pine, earth, and that male scent that only belonged to Devlin.

I jumped as a cloak was placed over my shoulders. I knew who it was even before I turned around. Devlin stood right behind me. My breath stuttered and left my body. He was so close. His hands lingered a moment, and his fingertips brushed my collarbone as he adjusted the cloak. "Can't have ye getting sick now that ye are finally healed from yer wound, now can we?" he whispered, his hands resting on my shoulders.

I couldn't answer. My eyes slowly trailed up the planes of his chest to the lines of his face. My heart raced, and the fire that had almost died out sprang to life, and began flowing through my veins. My body leaned into his and, when I reached his eyes, I saw unveiled passion staring down at me. His face was only inches from mine now. He leaned down toward me, his lips a heartbeat from mine. I smelled the ale on his breath, mixed with the scent that was only his. My body ached to be touched. I licked my lips. My eyes flicked to his mouth, and that's all he needed.

His mouth descended on mine, and my world flipped upside down.

I placed my hands on his chest to steady myself, but found them wandering over his chiseled muscles, tracing their lines, learning his body.

Devlin's lips devoured mine. His hands took possession, one encircling my neck, the other delving into my hair, undoing the braid Drea had so meticulously worked on. His lips caressed mine, then he nibbled, and coaxed me to open for him.

I did so willingly, and his tongue snaked out to taste me. It was hesitant at first, but more demanding as the kiss went on. Wrapping my arms around his neck, I melted into him, our tongues exploring, touching, and tasting every inch of our mouths. I needed to be closer to him, needed to touch him, and needed him to touch me. My breasts were heavy and sensitive, aching. My hands started roaming, trying to figure out how to divest him of his clothes. They were in my way. I needed to touch his skin.

Devlin deepened the kiss, changing the pace, building a rhythm with his tongue as his hands traveled along my spine, spreading wide, and pressing me against him. The evidence of his arousal was pushing against my stomach. He thrust against me, the same rhythm as his tongue. It only fueled my need to get rid of our clothing. Devlin tore himself away from my mouth and trailed kisses down the side of my neck to my collarbone, nipping along the way, and soothing those little bites with his tongue. I leaned my head to the side to give him better access, enjoying the feel of his lips and tongue on my bare skin. He trailed kisses up my neck, then found my lips once more, and kissed me tenderly. My emotions were on overload. I couldn't breathe, and I felt like I was floating on air.

Devlin leaned his forehead against mine, taking my hair into his hand again. "What shall I do with ye? Every time I am near ye, all I want to do is touch ye and taste ye, then wring yer little neck all at the same time." He kissed me again, roughly this time.

Before I could answer, Argus barreled at me, pushing me away from Devlin, barking at me incessantly. I tried to push him away, to get to Devlin, but he growled at me, turning me and backing me up the steps.

"Argus, stop it. Right now!"

He planted his butt right in front of me and I peeked at Devlin. His eyes spit fire, and he strode toward Argus.

I put my hand up. "Wait. Do you hear that?"

He stopped. He must have heard it then, because he looked in my eyes, fear showing for just a moment, before they locked down and became the eyes of the man I first met.

As we heard the call again, Devlin said, "Get inside, find Drea and my sister-in-law, and hide. Tell Christan I need him now!"

I stood there, gaping at him.

"Go, Jami, now!" He took off at a run toward the gates.

Devlin ran, yelling instructions as he went, and gathering men to meet the Mulligans. He yelled for the archers to man their posts along the walls, and to take out any bloody Mulligan they saw. With arrows flying, he and the rest of his men went through the gate to meet the threat head on, his guards closing and securing the gates behind them.

CHAPTER 19

I stood for another moment until Argus pushed against my legs. I sprinted into action, running into the keep, with Argus at my feet. I stopped to get my bearings, and scanned the room for Drea. She'd seen me come in and was already making her way to me.

"Jami, what's wrong?" she asked, concern written on her face.

"I have to find Christan. Devlin needs him now!"

Christan was steps away from me. When he saw my face, he hurried his pace. "Lady Jami, what is it? Is all well?" he asked in a hushed voice, so as not to alarm the others at the tables.

"Devlin needs you. We heard a call when we were outside. I'm not sure what it was, but it sounded like the warning call I heard you teaching the young men earlier."

Christan snapped his head up at my statement. "All right, Lady Jami, listen carefully. Go straight to yer room. Drea, get Emily and go with her. Ye three stay there until either Devlin or I come get ye." Christan strode toward Donovan.

Drea followed him to gather Emily.

I went to the stairs to wait for them.

Drea and Emily came out of the great hall at a fast pace, with Donovan and Christan right behind them. "Emily, get the little one and stay with the others till we return. Do not leave the room, and do not open the door for anyone but Christan, Devlin, or myself," Donovan instructed. He grabbed her in a fierce kiss, then followed Christan out the door.

Emily started up the stairs, with Drea and I fast on her heels. We ran to the nursery. Emily scooped her babe into her arms and we hurried to my room, and Argus followed behind us the whole way. Inside we locked the door. Emily finally stopped a minute and just held her child. I went to the windows to watch the madness in the courtyard. Drea stood beside me.

"What's going on?" I asked.

"The Mulligans are here. Devlin had a feeling they would attack soon, but we didn't think it would be this close after the Fall Festival," Emily answered.

"What do you mean attack?"

"They will try to breach the keep walls and steal our grain, our stock—anything they can get their hands on—and they will kill anyone who gets in their way. There are rumors they have enlisted someone or something to help them overtake us."

Drea placed her hand on my arm, and turned me to her. "Jami, don't worry. This is what Devlin and Christan train for every day. They have won every battle brought to this keep, and they will win this one."

My vision suddenly went grey. Drea was still holding my arm, but I was no longer in my chambers. I was in a field, with rain pouring down, and wind whipping around me. Bodies were strewn all around. I looked to my left and found Drea with me.

"Where are we?"

"I think we are sharing a vision, Jami. This is the field outside the keep walls."

"Who are all these men?"

"I don't know, but I see both O'Rourke and Mulligan tartans among them."

Tears formed in my eyes as I stared at the carnage. A high-pitched roar made us both turn toward the keep. At the gates, men fought, but just above them, a woman stood at a pair of windows thrown wide open. Her hair thrashed all around her, and she was dressed in a green velvet dress. Her arms were thrown to the heavens, and the winds picked up to almost hurricane levels.

It was me.

We held onto each other for dear life, watching as the winds picked up the Mulligan men and threw them about, taking down their forces one by one. The sky darkened, and bolts of lightning struck down around us. We huddled together, crouched down. I was afraid we were going to die. My fingers dug into Drea's arm, and my arm band started glowing bright green.

"Shh, all is well. It's a vision, and nothing can hurt us here. Let's see if we can find out who is calling the lightning." Just at the edge of the forest, we saw her.

Raven black hair flowed around her. She was dressed in battle gear, her arms raised to the sky, and her eyes aglow.

"There she is. Let's get closer. I want to see if I recognize her."

We crept up the hill, weaving through bodies, and holding on to each other against the winds, until we came upon her. We couldn't have been but twenty feet away when she turned and looked right at us. Her eyes were storm clouds, with lightning strikes making them glow in the dark.

"Ye will not win this time, sister. He will be mine."

Drea and I woke to find ourselves sitting against the wall below the windows.

Emily had set the babe down with Argus, and was shaking us. "Ye both scared the hell out of me. Where were ye?"

"It seems Jami can also share visions with me," Drea said, as she stood to pour us each a glass of water. "Emily, ye may want to sit down. We know who the Mulligans have on their side."

Emily sat with the little one, waiting for her to explain.

"Who was that, Drea? And what was she doing?"

Drea took a long drink. "I am not positive, but if the legend is correct, Jami, that is Blair. She would be yer twin sister."

I gasped.

"The legend goes, that after 200 years of living in the faery world, there would be a birth of twins. One would be allowed to rejoin the human realm, and the other would stay in faery to keep the bloodline going. That set of twins was born to yer parents, Jami. But the legend also tells that these two sisters will meet again and face each other. Only one will win, the fate of the clans will be held in their hands." With sadness in her eyes, Drea continued. "Jami, I am sorry, I thought we would have more time for ye to learn all of this, and to learn how to harness and control the powers ye have."

I stared at the fire, trying to absorb what Drea had just told me. "So she has powers too, and it seems like she has had more practice than I have." I began to shake, realizing this clan needed my help and I had no clue what I was doing.

"Yes, she does, but her powers are different. Ye see these children were born of light and dark, and so in turn their powers are such. Blair is of the dark. She can wield the power of fire and of storms as we saw. Ye have the power of light, the elements of earth, air, and water. Ye have more power in yer pinky than she has in her whole body, and she knows it. She also knows ye haven't grown up using them, and that is what she is trusting in, that ye will shy away from them and turn from those who need ye."

"I won't. I'll never shy away from you or your family. I know deep down that this is where I belong. I will do everything I can to help save this clan," I said, my voice strong with conviction.

Emily nodded. "I know ye will, Jami. I have faith in ye."

I straightened my shoulders and faced Drea. "So where do we start?"

"First ye need to embrace yer powers. My father told me yer parents harnessed their powers and bound them to something they would have passed on to ye. A talisman of some sort, and the way to unlock those powers would be written in yer family history."

I glanced at the stand by the bed. The box my parents had left me glowed around the edges. I walked over and lifted the lid. I heard the necklace humming louder than it'd ever hummed before, and it emanated a glow that lit the room. I lifted it and hooked the clasp behind my neck. As it settled at my collarbone, the glow subsided and the necklace warmed on my skin. I placed its box on the bed, and opened the case where my book was stored. I faced Drea with it in my hands. "This is the book that came to me, and so far what I've read is my history. But I haven't read it all. I don't know where to search to find out how to release my parents' powers."

This was all a bit surreal. I had to be dreaming, right? I wouldn't normally just accept this without question. *Must be a dream*, but my cuff buzzed against my bicep and I knew I had to face it. This was really happening, and these two women were counting on me to save the clan. Could I do this? Little Jami Morgan? Or perhaps I should say Jami O'Malley, if this book were to be believed. I didn't know, but I had to try.

I sat across from Drea. "Now what?"

"Let it show ye," she said.

I gazed at the book in my hands. I sat it spine down in my lap, held both covers, and took a deep breath. "Show me."

I let go of the covers.

The book fell open to a passage I hadn't read yet. It was titled *Destiny Reveals All*. I started reading and, right there in front of me, were instructions from my parents on how to harness both their powers and mine fully. "Drea, I need my other case, please."

She grabbed it from the bed and placed it on the floor to my right. I read the passage again, and placed my right hand on the symbol carved into the top of the case. My left hand snaked around the cover of my book, finding the design embossed on the leather. I placed the final finger, and both symbols warmed beneath my hands.

"Reveal to me now, the destiny that is mine."

A surge went through me. It traveled up my arms, through my veins, down my chest, and flowed until it filled me fully. It slowly settled down to a mild hum throughout my body. "Drea, I need your help now."

I reached both my hands out to hers, realizing they were warmer than normal. "I need to see my history, and I need you to ground me here, according to the book. It's the last thing I have to do before I will fully understand my powers." I shook my head. Did I really believe this? I stared at my hands. Yeah, I did.

Drea took my hands in hers, then I found myself sitting in a glen. I slowly stood and gazed around, trying to get my bearings. I saw two people on the other side of the field. I walked around the edge, trying to get close enough to see who they were. As soon as I was close enough, the female smiled up at me. "Jami, we have been waiting for ye."

It struck me then, these were my parents. My birth parents.

My father beamed at me. "Ye have grown into quite the young woman. Remember we always loved ye. But we don't have much time, so listen carefully. Ye already know about yer twin sister and yer powers. The key to controlling yer powers is to listen to yer heart, open yerself up, and accept the gifts the elements give ye. Treat them with respect, and only use them when absolutely necessary.

"That is one thing yer sister could never learn. From the moment she realized she could wield the elements, she used them for personal reasons, and did not respect them. For that, she was stripped of all but two powers, though she has developed them over the years into the two most dangerous."

"Be careful around Blair. She cares for no one but herself, and she wants yer Devlin. She has seen a future with him that has her in control of all the lands. She wants that desperately, and is willing to hurt anyone who gets in her way," my mother said.

Both my mother and father gazed over my shoulder.

"Our time is up, Jami," my father said with sadness etched in his face.

I turned my head to see what had caught their attention.

A tall man stood in the middle of the glen. He was wearing robes of silver and gold. His hair was long, and a crown sat atop his head. I started to ask my parents who he was, but they were gone. I stood and faced the man.

"Hello, Jamison." He greeted me in a voice that carried a melodic tone that made the birds around us sing, and drew the animals of the glen out of hiding. "You don't know me, but you carry my blood within your veins. Heed your parent's advice, my child, and you will live a long and happy life. But doubt yourself even a little bit, and you risk losing it all."

I didn't realize he'd moved toward me till he stopped speaking. He was right in front of me.

"I can't interfere in the battle, but I can help you in a small way." He touched my dress, right above the symbol that had appeared in my skin, and muttered a few words under his breath.

My skin heated and a prickling sensation ran down my spine.

"A small bit of protection." He gazed into my eyes. "Be safe, my child." He waved his hand over my eyes to close them, and was gone.

Drea pulled on my hands. "Jami, wake up. Ye have to return to us."

I scanned the room as the vision faded.

Drea took me to the window "It's started, Jami."

CHAPTER 20

I looked out the window to see the men from both sides starting to fall in the fields of heather outside the keep walls. I turned to Drea. "Help me change, quickly." We both found Emily holding up a simple gown in green, with long flowing arms, and a band of wide ribbon right under the bust.

"I had a dream ye would need this, Jami," Emily said with tears in her eyes. We quickly changed the dresses, removing the constricting corset in the process. My shoes were left under the bed. I checked both women and went to the open windows.

I gazed upon the fields, the clash of broadswords and yells of the men meeting my ears. "Emily, take the little one to the other side of the bed and stay on the floor with him. Do not come out for any reason." Argus came to stand by my side. "Argus, you stay with them too, protect the little one for me." He nudged my hand and whined, so I patted him and he went to do as I'd instructed. "Drea, stay near. I may have need of you."

She nodded.

I climbed up on the wide windowsill, and closed my eyes. Focusing on each breath, I calmed and opened myself to the powers that lay within. The cuff on my arm and the pendant at my neck began to warm my skin and hum in time with my heart. I raised my arms shoulder high, tilted my head, and heard my parents' voices on the wind.

We are with you always.

It was time. The energy pooled in my blood and, with open eyes, I released my breath. Turning my palms outward, I focused on the battle unfolding before me. I asked the winds for their help in protecting my clan, my family, and my life.

The wind caressed my face, and whispered in my hair as it

attacked those doing harm to the men I now considered my family. Instinctively, I closed my eyes and envisioned the winds throwing the Mulligans around, forcing them to turn in fear, lifting them away, and being the driving force against their attack. My eyes opened to see many of the Mulligans slowed greatly, but others were still advancing. I raised my arms to the sky, asking the clouds to open and release their rain, using the wind to whip it around, and picking up debris and rock to combine into weapons of my own. I directed the elements with my thoughts, power surging out of me, and drove them up the hillside, allowing our men to take advantage and pursue them.

The skies darkened, thunderheads rolled in, and lightning struck the field of battle, scorching the earth and pushing our men to the safety of the wall. I called Drea to me. Without turning to her, I asked, "Can you find her? I feel her out there, but I can't pinpoint her location. Can you tell if she is still at the edge of the forest? If I don't take her out, we don't have a chance at survival."

"I think I can. My sight will allow me to search for a short time." Drea sat in front of the fire.

I continued to direct the winds and rain, helping our men any way I could, by throwing rocks and small boulders in the path of the Mulligan warriors. An eternity seemed to pass before Drea came to me. My strength was waning. This had to stop now, before I exhausted not only my powers, but my body completely. "Did you find her?"

"Yes," she said and breathed. I heard the strain in her voice. "She is just beyond the tree line, to the left of the path leading to the gates. I can show ye."

I nodded.

Drea grasped my ankle and pushed a picture into my mind, the exact spot she saw Blair. She released me and collapsed to the floor below me.

"Thank you, Drea." I closed my eyes and, with my right hand, gestured to the group of trees surrounding Blair. I called to the trees and asked for their help. I envisioned their branches bending toward her outstretched hands, scraping at her. Their roots surfacing to encase her legs, and the ivy travelling up her body and wrapping around her, binding her arms to her sides. I directed the ivy to continue up and wrap around her head, blindfolding her, and providing a gag to keep her from casting any more spells.

When I opened my eyes, the lightning had stopped. I focused again on pushing the Mulligans to retreat. When they realized they no longer had help from Blair, they tucked tail and ran. The cheers from our men rang out in the night. I raised my hands and pushed the winds up into the clouds, breaking them up, and allowing a calm to settle over the field as the moon was revealed.

I found Devlin at the gates, his broadsword raised in triumph. That was the last thing I saw, my body exhausted, and my powers drained. My vision went black and I fell to the floor.

With sword raised and Christan by his side, they dove into the chaos, meeting the intruders head on, swinging and slicing their way through the throng. He saw man after man go down and, after the first few, he couldn't tell if they were his or Mulligan's. Only one man would be foolish enough to lead a raid this close to winter, and it was that man he was after. Jakob Mulligan, the youngest of the Mulligan sons.

Devlin took down man after man, stepping over bodies in search of Jakob. Quickly glancing around, he saw Christan, Bran, Connor, and Declan had things well in hand, leading their men to what could only be a victory. He searched the sea of warriors, finding Jakob near the rear, shouting orders. The coward.

"We've got this, Devlin, go get the bastard."

Devlin faced another swarm of men coming toward them. Realizing his men were scattered, he yelled for them to fall back and regroup. He hated that this took him further from Jakob, but the lives of his men were more important right now. Then the winds picked up and seemed to be attacking Mulligan's men, whipping them to and fro, and picking them up and throwing them around. He realized his men were not affected, then turned and found the source of this magic. He saw a figure in a window of the keep, her arms outstretched, and her head tilted to the sky. Her hair and dress were whipping about her. His body already knew who it was, and his heart skipped a few beats. "Jami," he whispered. She seemed to emanate a faint green glow. Her head came up and the rains started.

Turning to the fight, he yelled, "Move them back, and take every Mulligan that ye can. FOR CLAN O'ROURKE!" As one, they moved forward, striking down every man in their path. Devlin didn't know how she was doing it, but he wasn't going to worry about it now. There would be time for that later. Right now, he needed to get to Jakob.

It was as if the winds heard him, and a path opened up straight to Jakob at the crest of the hill. He ran toward him and, as he reached the top, a bolt of lightning struck the ground right in front of him, throwing him. While lying there sprawled in the field, his ears ringing from the blast, he saw more lightning strike the earth around him. It scattered his men, giving the Mulligans the advantage again. He stood and turned toward Jakob, only to find he was no longer there. Turning in a circle quickly, he tried to locate him, but couldn't find him anywhere.

Seeing Christan to his left, flanked by three Mulligans, he went to aid his best friend. He went up behind them and took two out before they realized he was there. Christan dispatched of the third. "Thanks, but I could have handled them."

"Of that, I have no doubt, but I need yer assistance. I feel Jakob has run," Devlin yelled over the din of clashing swords and booming thunder.

"We will find him, Devlin. He will pay for this," Christan assured as they faced another group of Mulligans.

Suddenly, the lightning stopped. Devlin's men forged on, cutting down the Mulligans' forces. They saw Jakob at the crest of the hill, astride his horse and calling for his men to retreat. Those that were left standing retreated over the hill into the trees. A few of Devlin's men followed, forcing them past the boundaries of O'Rourke land. Devlin and Christan gathered the rest of the men and sent them to the keep, instructing them to take those that needed medical attention to the Great Hall. When he saw his men standing there, exhausted but triumphant, he raised his broadsword and let out a whoop of victory. "Clan O'Rourke!" he yelled.

His eyes were pulled to the figure of Jami outlined in the window and, even at this distance, he swore he caught her eye. He sensed her, and he knew something was wrong. As he continued to watch, she fell backward out of sight.

Devlin's heart stopped.

With a sick feeling in his stomach, he instructed, "Christan, take Bran, Connor, and Declan, and get the men into the keep. Help those who can't walk on their own, and make sure to send a scouting party out to patrol the rest of the night."

He took off at a run toward the keep, his heart constricting at the thought that something was wrong with Jami.

He burst through the keep doors and took the stairs two at a time, coming to a stop at the door to Jami's chambers. He pounded on the door until Emily opened it. Stepping out of his way, Emily let him in. He scanned the room and found Drea sitting beside Jami on the bed. Walking, still covered in the mud, grime, and dried blood from battle, he stared down at Jami while Emily tried to comfort her little one. He must have been a scary sight, but he had to reassure himself that Jami was all right.

Drea looked at him. "She will be fine, Lord Devlin. She just needs to rest. She used up her energy helping ye fight. She should be fine by morning."

He didn't acknowledge Drea as she got up from the bed. He simply knelt down next to Jami, scanning her face, and watching her chest rise and fall with each breath. Leaning in, he whispered, "Thank ye; I don't know what or how ye did it, but if it weren't for ye, I feel we would have lost. If I ever see ye putting yerself in danger like that again, I'll take a strap to ye myself. We will talk about this on the morrow."

He swept an errant strand of hair off her forehead and, with one last glance, he strode from the room.

CHAPTER 21

Devlin made his way out the front door of the keep. He needed to get to his men, assess the damage, and help those wounded. But in the mood he was in, he'd be no good to them. He walked around the side of the keep, then began pacing the length, and trying to calm his rapidly-beating heart. He was sick to his stomach, thinking of what could've happened to Jami. His body shook with a rage at her for putting herself in that position. He was so upset that he didn't hear Drea run up behind him.

"Devlin." She stopped. "Devlin, stop. There is someone ye need to attend to"

"Who? That coward Mulligan has run off."

"Not Mulligan. It's who was helping him. Jami just woke and told me she's still tied up in the trees. It's draining Jami, keeping her imprisoned. Ye need to get her before Jami's energy is depleted and she gets away. I can show ye where she is. Hurry, we don't have much time." Drea grabbed Devlin's hand.

Devlin felt the shock before the vision overtook him. Drea showed him the way before he jerked his hand from hers.

"Let's go." Devlin strode off, Drea having to run to keep up with him. "Christan, grab some rope and come with me." They barreled past the barracks.

Christan grabbed the supplies and jogged to catch up.

"Where are we going, Devlin? We have men to tend to," Christan questioned.

"There is still someone ye need to question. Jami has her bound up in the tree line, but her strength is leaving her fast. If we don't get there quick, Blair will get away," Drea said.

"Who's Blair?" Christan asked

"It's who the Mulligans had helping them, and she is Jami's

sister, twin to be exact."

Devlin and Christan picked up their pace. As they approached the tree line, Devlin gestured to Drea. "Where is she?"

Drea took the lead and brought them to the exact spot where Blair was still bound by the roots and ivy.

"How are we supposed to get her out of that?" Christan snorted. As if the vines had heard him, they started to loosen.

Devlin was behind her in an instant, grasping her wrists as they were released.

"What the hell do ye think ye are doing? Let me go, ye animals. Ye have no idea who ye are dealing with. Ye will pay for this." Blair scanned the group, her eyes black as night, and latching onto Drea.

"And ye. Ye little bitch, are ye the one who did this to me? How—"

Devlin promptly replaced the vines that had loosened from her mouth with a linen rag, effectively gagging her again. With her hands secure, the roots released her legs.

"Christan, take this wench to the dungeons. We will speak with her after our men are taken care of," Devlin instructed.

Christan tied her ankles and threw her over his shoulder, having obvious trouble keeping the squirming woman in place.

Devlin's gaze bore down on Drea. "Now explain to me how this woman is related to Jami."

"I wish I had the time, but I think that's something Jami herself would want to tell ye. I must return to her. Now that she has released all the elements, I need to make sure she is all right." Drea ran toward the keep.

"Why the hell won't anyone tell me what is going on?" Devlin shook his head. He made his way to the keep, surveying the fields that used to be ripe with heather, but now resembled a mass grave, the spilled blood of his enemy and his own men mingling to tinge the fields a brownish red. He made a note to form a group to take care of the bodies as soon as possible. He didn't want his clan to see this devastation.

He saw a few families out gathering their fallen warriors, taking them home to give them a proper send off and burial. The family cemetery would be adding more than one headstone this season. It broke his heart to see so many men's lives taken for reasons unknown to him. He didn't know what Jakob Morgan was up to, but he'd find out.

CHAPTER 22

I awoke to find Drea sitting next to me.

"Finally, she wakes. Ye gave us quite the scare," she greeted with a smile.

"What time is it?" I asked. "How long have I been asleep?"

"Almost two days. The fight took much out of ye, and yer body and spirit needed to regenerate."

"What?" I sat up quickly, the room spinning around me. I grabbed my head as my stomach made it known to all in the room that I was hungry.

"Take it easy. We need to get some food in ye, to build yer strength up. I think after a good meal, ye will be right as rain," Drea said as she got up to go instruct a servant to fetch a tray for me.

"What about Blair? Did they find her? Did she get away?"

"I led Devlin and Christan to where ye had her trapped before exhaustion overtook ye. They have her locked in the dungeon, but she says she won't talk to anyone but ye. They did at least take my advice and put her in the cell encased in iron. She is under tight security as well. Right now eat and rest so that ye can get on yer feet. I think Devlin wants to speak with ye before ye see Blair. He has lots of questions of his own."

I dropped my head into my hands. "I'm sure he does, but I don't know if I have the answers for him. I'm not even sure what happened, or how I did it."

Argus nudged my hand to get attention.

I scratched his head. "Where the hell have you been, boy? You stink to high heaven. You most definitely need a bath," I told him as I crinkled my nose.

A knock sounded at the door and Drea answered to find the servant carrying a tray heavily laden with food. She allowed him to enter and place the tray on the table in front of the fire. After seeing him to the door, she came to help me out of bed, into my dressing gown, and over to the chairs. I was famished, and the smell of food only fueled my hunger. I sat down and dove into my food, not caring what I looked like.

When I finished, my belly was satisfied, so I sat with a mug of warm cider and relaxed. I was starting to feel better, and the fire did wonders to warm me up. As I wound down, I realized how gross I felt, as though I was caked with dirt and grime. I sighed. "Do you think it's possible for me to get a bath before I have to see Devlin? I feel dirty, and am sure I smell worse than I feel."

"Absolutely, why don't ye go sit by the window. I'll have this cleared away and the tub brought in. It shouldn't take long to fill, as the kitchens always have water on to boil."

I nodded and, with Drea's help, moved my chair to the window so I could see out over the courtyard and watch the daily buzz. People moved about in their daily chores, and the children were running and playing.

Argus came over to sit next to me.

"Hey boy, why don't you go out and play with the kids? You've been cooped up in here for too long."

He barked and took off out the door.

I looked out the window in time to see him bounding down the steps and running straight for a little boy who seemed to be outside the circle of kids playing. A smile formed on my lips. He'd found a kindred spirit, someone like him, outside the circle. It lightened my heart to see how he made the child laugh and smile.

When the servants came in, I made my way toward the fire. A nice hot bath was being filled for me. I slowly walked over to the tub.

"Would ye like help?" Drea inquired.

I shook my head. "I think I can handle it, thank you."

I dropped my dressing gown and nightrail as I slipped into the steaming water. I sighed as I sank down, the water an almost-scalding temperature. I soaked for a few minutes, before taking the wash cloth and soap and scrubbing the dirt and grime of the last few days away. I washed my hair as best I could, then just let the warmth of the water seep into my bones and ease the ache of my muscles. When the water started to cool, I stood and stepped out, grabbing the towels that had been draped by the fire to warm. I sat on the stool placed there and started drying my hair, running my fingers through it to separate the strands and untangle the knots.

When my body was dried, I went to the wardrobe and picked out a simple day dress, and put it on with a pair of warm wool tights. I moved my chair by the fire, planning to relax with my hair hanging near it to dry, but a knock at my door stopped me before I could sit down. I opened the door to find the same servant who'd brought my food standing there. I let him in to remove the cold water and the bath tub. I sat and watched him as he worked.

He reminded me a bit of Devlin, his muscles moving beneath his tunic as he emptied the tub and removed it from the room. Thoughts of Devlin invaded my mind as I relaxed by the fire. I let my eyes drift shut and my imagination took over. Visions of Devlin half dressed filled my mind, his body covered in sweat, not from a workout in the lists, but from the anticipation of a workout with me. I took the daydream further, imagining what he looked like fully naked, stalking toward me in all his glory, with eyes only for me. My body heated at the thought. My core was throbbing, my breasts were aching, and I licked my lips in anticipation.

Someone cleared their throat near me and my eyes shot open. Heat crept up my neck as I realized what I'd been doing. My legs had dropped open and my hands had started easing their way down my body, trying to fulfill the ache I had. I sat straight to find Devlin standing in my doorway. I tried to calm my racing heart. His face told me he could tell what I'd been imagining. My face warmed, but it hadn't stopped at my neck. My cheeks were aflame with heat.

"Am I interrupting anything?" He smirked.

"No, not at all." I indicated the other chair in the room. "Would you like to sit down?"

Devlin walked over and sat, his frame seeming to dwarf the dainty chair. "I have a few things to discuss with ye, and some questions I need answered." He gazed into my eyes.

I broke eye contact and stared at the floor. "I will do my best to answer them."

This was not a conversation I was looking forward to, especially since I found it hard to concentrate. My body vibrated with the need to go over and just curl up in Devlin's lap, kissing him till his mind went blank and his body took over.

"What the hell happened three nights ago?"

"That is when we were almost invaded." I smiled at him.

"I have no need for yer sass. I mean what did ye do? I saw ye at this window, and then the wind and rain and earth started moving as if they were helping us fight."

"They were. I called on them to help. I can't really explain how. I'm not truly sure how I did it myself, but I trusted my instincts, followed my heart, and it just came to me." I shook my head. "I know that's not what you were wanting to hear, but it's the only way I can put it into words. I could show you, but you don't believe. I can't share my memory or feelings with someone if they don't believe."

"I believe something happened, but it feels more like some type of witchcraft to me."

My eyes widened. He believed what he said. I read it on his face. "Witchcraft? I'm not a witch," I replied, sitting straighter and glaring at him. "I can't explain exactly what happened. I called with my heart and soul, and the elements answered. It was not witchcraft; no spells were done, and nothing was sacrificed. I did it to save you and your clan, who are like family to me."

I stood and started pacing. Devlin was pissing me off. I almost died helping, and he thinks me some witch. My anger built until my blood was boiling. Devlin was staring wide eyed into the fire. The flames had tripled in size, and were licking the inside of the chimney.

He swung his wide-eyed gaze to me. I walked toward him, and the flames leapt from the fire toward me. When an ember leapt out and singed the carpet, I realized the flames were responding to my anger. I stopped, took a cleansing breath and, with my hand, gestured for the flames to lower. Instantly, the fire returned to normal.

"See? No spells, no incantations, and no spoken words. I honestly didn't even realize I was controlling the flames. They just responded to my emotions, I guess. I didn't even think fire was an element I had control over." I flopped down in my chair, letting my head fall. "Guess I was wrong. This is all new to me, and I learn more each day. It's hard and a struggle to have all of this just dumped on me. No training and no instructions on how to control or use it."

I heard Devlin's shallow breaths, but still he said nothing.

I opened my eyes. "You said you had questions to ask me. What else do you want to know? I'm getting tired, and would really like to get this over with."

I noticed his gaze glued to my neck, then traveling down and up the length of me, before settling on my eyes. He fidgeted in his seat a bit. He wasn't only trying to wrap his head around what had just happened. He was reacting to our physical attraction as well, if the bulge in his pants was any indication. I was glad to know he wasn't immune to the sparks flying between us.

"This woman we have in the dungeon, Drea said she is yer sister, and she says the same. Who is she?"

"That is another story I don't have all the details to. Drea and I have been pouring over my family history book. Between that and a vision she and I shared, I figured out she is my sister. My twin, in fact, but she was left in the Fae realm, and raised with the full knowledge of her powers. She was taught how to harness, use, and control them. But sometime in her life she started using them for self-gain and with evil intentions.

"According to the legend, my parents were destined to have a set of twins. One would be allowed in the human realm and one would stay in the realm of the Fae. Obviously, I was sent to the human realm. I don't know why, and I haven't been able to locate my parents to ask them. They were bound to silence until my twenty-fifth birthday, when everything went to hell and I was transported here."

Facing Devlin, I said, "I know you probably think me insane, but you wanted the truth, and that's what I'm trying to give you. You know deep down I'm not lying. I can see it in your eyes. You won't let yourself believe it because it doesn't make sense, and you can't rationally explain what I've done or what's happened.

"Believing me will take faith and trust, and that doesn't come easily to you, I know."

Devlin stood to pace in front of the fire, his agitation apparent in the way he carried himself. "This is all so farfetched. Ye say ye are from a future time, and sometimes I want to believe ye. Some of the things ye say, how ye act, it all seems out of place. Then other times ye fit right in. I don't know what to believe. Faith was never something I carried well. I left the faith and belief to my father and, when he died, what little faith I had died with him. Now here ye are telling me to have faith, to believe what I cannot see or feel, and I find it hard. Deep down, something keeps urging me to, but if I let go and rely on faith ..."

He shook his head. "It's asking too much. I just can't."

"I know it's hard, Devlin, but listen to your heart. You can't deny the attraction between us, and it's more than just physical. I feel complete when I'm with you, and that scares the hell out of me, but I have faith in my instincts. You need to dig deep and open yourself. It's scary and uncomfortable, but it's the only way, and you will help save your clan. This thing between you and the Mulligans isn't over. To defeat them, we will need to be united. If not, my sister will win, and that's not a future you want to have." I stood to go to Devlin and the room spun.

Devlin was beside me in a flash, catching me before I hit the floor. "I have taken too much time. I can see ye still need to rest. I will leave ye." He helped me to sit down.

"I need to speak with my sister soon, Devlin. Can you arrange for me to be taken down to see her?"

"I don't think that's wise. We don't know what she's capable of," he declined.

"She won't hurt me, not yet anyway. I know it, I can feel it here." I tapped my chest. "She wants to meet me, see what I am capable of. I need to do the same."

Devlin hesitated, deep in thought. With a sigh, he agreed. "Very well, but ye must rest first. I'll come this afternoon and escort ye myself."

"Thank you."

Devlin walked out, his shoulders hunched.

I couldn't help but admire his retreating figure. He really did have a nice ass.

I made my way to the bed. I really was tired. A nap would do me good before I met my sister for the first time.

This time my dreaming found me in the keep. I wandered around, watching the hustle and bustle of daily life happening. I saw Christan and decided to follow him. He seemed to be heading to a section of the keep I had yet to explore. I followed him down hallways that got darker and darker, until he stopped at a door. He extracted a key from his belt and unlocked it. I followed him into the landing just inside as he closed the door.

"I don't know who ye are, but I know ye are there," Christan said.

I gasped, he couldn't know, could he? No one had ever known I was there before.

"My gran had a bit of gypsy in her. I can feel ye and I know ye are female by the smell of yer soap. Lilac and heather I believe." He grinned. "Ye can speak to me, I'll hear ye. I don't want to hurt ye, just curious as to who is following me."

I stepped around to face him. His eyes scanned the landing, but he didn't see me. "Christan, can you really her me?"

I held my breath.

"Lady Jami?" he whispered. "How?"

"That's something I intend to find out, Christan. Sometimes in my dreams, I wander. Today is one of those times. Oh, and please just call me Jami. If you can sense and hear me, I think that puts us on a level of friends."

"I would like that, Jami, to be yer friend. I know it's hard for Devlin to believe what is happening, but I want to let ye know that I am grateful for what ye did to help us the other night, and if ye ever need anything, ye let me know."

"Christan, I need to see my sister. I know Devlin said he would escort me later today, but I need to talk to her before then. Can you take me to her? I don't know if I'll be able to communicate with her, but I need to see her."

"Jami, I really shouldn't. If Devlin finds out, he will kick my arse and then lock ye away in a tower till he sees fit to let ye out." Christan laughed. "I would love to see that fight, though."

I tried to kick him, but my foot just went through his leg. Damn this ghostly form.

"Hey, that tickled. Did ye just touch me?" Christan asked

"No, I tried to kick you, but it didn't work, obviously."

Christan snorted. "I see I won't be able to talk ye out of this, so follow me, I'll take ye to her cell. But be forewarned, she is encased in iron bars. Ye may not be able to speak with her. The one thing I do know is iron will prohibit the use of her powers, and it may yers as well."

"All right, noted. Now can we get on with it? I don't know how long I'll sleep."

Christan started down a flight of stairs, taking the torch from the landing to light the way. The stairs led down to a dark, musty and moldy dungeon. Doors lined the wall and, at the very end, was a cell made entirely of iron bars.

Blair paced the length of it.

"There she is, Jami. I can only take ye this far," Christan whispered.

I peered down the rest of the hall and saw why. There were three guards sitting at a table not far from the cell. I recognized Bran among them. I walked passed Christan, brushing his cheek with my hand in thanks.

He raised his hand, touching his cheek in wonder.

I walked all the way up to the cell, waiting to see if she'd notice I was there.

She stared right at me. *So ye finally came to see me.* Her lips didn't move. It took me a moment to realize she'd spoken to me in my thoughts.

"You can see me?" I asked out loud.

"Of course I can. We are of the same blood, remember? These bars inhibit my active powers, but they don't harm my inactive powers. Like seeing through glamour, and being able to speak to yer mind. Ye know, ye can do this too. If ye just try." She smirked.

She didn't look like the same person I'd entrapped three nights ago. There was no evil pouring from her. It was like staring at a mirror image of me, only with raven black hair. Almost innocent.

"Why are you here? What is it you want?" I asked her.

The same thing ye want. I want my destiny. I heard in my thoughts again.

I shook my head. "I don't understand."

Of course ye wouldn't. Our parents thought it best to save ye, whisk ye away to some future time. Keep ye from our history, hoping this destiny wouldn't come about. But they were wrong. They chose ye to save, thinking I would die as the sacrifice to keep ye safe and happy. But that didn't happen. I grew. I became strong. I learned all I could. Oh, sister of mine, ye have so much to learn and very little time to do so. Ye see, we are halves of the same whole. Our destinies are intertwined. As twins, we share a soul, and we also share a soul mate.

Do ye understand what that means, dear sister? One soul cannot survive in two bodies. I am obviously the stronger of us, and I plan to have our soul mate. He is mine and ye won't stand in my way. Her eyes flashed with the storms that had consumed them the night of the raid. The iron bars sparked and Blair grabbed her head in pain.

"Ye can try all ye want. Yer powers won't help ye in there," Bran called down the hall, not glancing away from his cards.

I stared at Blair again, trying the whole mind speak for the first time. *Good luck with that. He doesn't believe in our powers. He thinks it's witchcraft. So I wish you luck on winning him over. Plus, the whole trying to destroy his clan didn't earn you any brownie points either.*

Blair laughed. *I don't care about winning him over, sister. He just has to be mine. I don't care if I have to bind him and put him in the dungeons for life. Ye don't understand, do ye? I suppose not, since ye weren't raised with the legends and prophecies. Let me explain it, dear. For the one sister who finds true love, who finds her soul mate, all powers become hers. Ye see, we weren't meant to be two. We were meant to be one child. When Fate decided to have some fun, our soul was split and twins were born. We aren't meant to stay this way; only one will gain all the powers. When true love is and the powers are transferred, the losing sister will wither and die.*

My eyes widened.

Yes, dear sister, one of us will die. So prepare yerself, because I will have Devlin and yer powers. She cackled out loud, bringing the attention of the guards.

I stepped back against the wall as they came to check on Blair.

I noticed something scurry along the wall. At first I thought it just a rat, until it glanced at me. Drea's eyes bore into mine. I needed to speak with her, but didn't want Christan hearing, as he was still down here waiting to walk up and let me out. Even in this form, I couldn't walk through doors or walls.

I wondered if speaking to someone's mind would work with Drea. I focused on her eyes. *Drea, I need to speak with you, meet me in my chambers.*

She squeaked, then ran up the dark hall and disappeared.

I walked near Christan. "Thank you. It's time for me to go."

He simply nodded. "Bran, ye report to Devlin if anything should change. Either he or I will check when it's time to change the guard."

Bran nodded and went to the card game the three of them had going.

Christan headed up the stairs, and I followed.

Outside the door, I whispered, "Thank you, Christan. I will see you at evening meal." I headed to my room.

He closed and locked the door behind me.

When I reached my chambers, I saw my body sleeping, but no sign of Drea. Maybe I could get a few more minutes of dreamless sleep before she arrived. I closed my eyes, and drifted into my body before complete darkness overtook me.

CHAPTER 23

I woke up later to find Drea sitting in the chair by the fire.

"Good afternoon, sleepy head. I came as soon as I could, but ye were sleeping soundly. I didn't want to wake ye, so I thought I would review some of the things my father gave me to read. Hopefully, I can help ye figure out what ye need to do."

I sat up. "Thank you, Drea. I assume you heard some of what she told me?"

She nodded. "I don't know how, but we are linked while ye sleep. I can see and hear what ye do, so yes, I heard everything. That's why I am reading. I don't remember that part of the story, but I seem to have found it in this book." She showed me the page. "Ye have until the second full moon after the invasion to find and capture the heart of yer soul mate, or yer powers will be forfeited to the stronger sister."

"And right now that seems to be Blair. Only two months. That doesn't seem long enough to convince Devlin."

"At the rate ye are going, no. But I have an idea."

I inclined my head for her to continue.

"Appealing to him to have faith and trust his heart doesn't seem to work, so why don't we appeal to his more basic needs? We know he desires ye. It's evident in the way he kisses ye. We need to prey on that, let his body lead his heart, instead of the other way around. He'll be yers before ye know it." Drea giggled.

"I don't know, Drea. I haven't a clue as to how to seduce a man. Plus, I don't know if I could control myself enough to accomplish it. I seem to go to putty when he's around. How am I supposed to think clearly and play coy when all I want to do is strip him naked and jump him?" I blushed.

"I think we need to get Emily involved. I know Donovan wasn't an easy catch. She can help us," Drea said with a mischievous glint in her eye.

I sighed. "All right, but I have a feeling I'm going to regret agreeing to this. I wish Todd were here. He'd know what to do."

"Who's Todd?" Drea asked.

"He is, or well, was, my best friend." I lay on the bed again, staring at the canopy above me. Thinking of Todd brought tears to my eyes. I missed him. I wondered what he was doing, and if he missed me as much.

Drea walked over and sat next to me on the bed.

"I keep forgetting a lot of this is new and different for ye. It must be hard being away from everyone ye know, but please remember I am here for ye and will help ye any way I can."

I squeezed her hand. "I know, and I really appreciate it." I took a deep breath. "Let's get Emily. The sooner we start, the sooner we can get this destiny thing over with and make sure our families are safe."

Drea nodded and fetched a servant to find Emily and bring her to us.

Emily was a fountain of knowledge. We explained our plan to seduce Devlin. She was eager to help, and called her seamstress immediately to start alterations on most of my dresses. She planned a few more gowns to be made; gowns more revealing and more tailored than those I already owned.

"It's all about showing just enough to entice them, but not too much as to reveal all yer assets. A tighter waist, slightly-lowered neckline and, of course, ye will have to be fitted for a new corset. We want to keep everything in its place for display." She was so giddy with excitement. I simply stood and let them measure every inch of my body. She and Todd would have gotten along well.

Emily went to the seamstress. "Can ye have this one altered and ready for evening meal?" The lady nodded and whisked the dress away with her to get started. Emily returned to me. "The corset won't be ready in time for evening meal, but I don't think ye will need it with that dress. The stays in the dress should be enough when the alterations are done. The next thing we must do is appeal to his sense of smell. I notice Devlin smells yer hair when ye are near; which soap are ye using?"

"The lilac and heather. It soothes me," I responded.

"Very well, I have some creams with the same scent. We must moisturize ye and infuse every pore with the scent. Not too heavily, just a light amount will do." She reached over to the basket she'd brought with her, and removed a jar of white cream that smelled exactly like the soap I used in my baths. "Slather this all over yer skin right before ye dress tonight, and he won't be able to resist ye between the scent and the dress. He'll be following ye around like a puppy before ye know it." She grinned.

I couldn't help but giggle at the image her words brought to mind. Devlin panting after me. Yeah, I wanted that, and so much more. I took the cream from her. "Thank you, Emily. You don't know how much I appreciate this."

"Oh, it's nothing. I haven't had a good girl's session in so long. This means as much to me as it does ye. Now we need to go for a walk. He needs to see ye out and about, talking with his people, maybe even flirting a little bit. Put this day dress on. It has the lowest neckline, and the waist fits perfectly. It will give him something to think about."

We made our way down and out the front door of the keep. It was a bit chilly, so Emily lent me one of her mantles again. This one wasn't as bulky, and flowed around my curves with slits where my arms fit through. We walked around the courtyard and made our way through the gardens, coming across the guard posted at the door.

Emily stopped a passing squire. "Landon, can ye tell me where Lord Devlin is?"

"He's out riding the borders, yer ladyship," Landon replied.

Emily smiled at me. "It's a beautiful day for a ride. Shall we start yer riding lessons?"

"I would love to, but I'd like to visit the cliffs first. I want to see if the sea responds to me again, or if it was a fluke before."

Emily nodded, and led us out of the gardens toward the cliffs. I took the mantle off and handed it to Drea. "Keep me safe and watch out for me. Ground me if needed."

She nodded, handed Emily my mantle, and walked with me to the end of the grass.

I walked out onto the rock ledge alone, breathing the salty air and tilting my head to the sky. I cleared my head and opened myself to the power of the elements. The blood in my veins hummed, and my hands started to tingle. The wind picked up and I raised my hands to the sky, my fingers wide open. I asked the seas to come and greet me.

The surf pounded the rocks below. I lowered my head and gazed out across the water, watching the waves reach to the sky, then fall upon themselves. The pounding of the waves slowly became the rhythm of my heart, they were becoming one with my spirit. I wanted to play a little, and pushed both hands in front of me, watching the water as it followed my reach, receding from the rocks. I raised my hands quickly to the sky and pulled them down to my sides. The sea responded, waves crashing hard against the side of the cliff below me, and the spray rising up in front of me, before falling to either side.

I glanced at Drea and Emily, a smile lighting my face. Over their shoulders, I saw him. Sitting astride a horse, just up the hill from where we stood, watching me.

I faced Drea and Emily, knowing Devlin could see me from where he sat. I raised my hands slowly to the sky, my head falling back as I did so. I slowed my breathing and silently thanked the sea for playing with me, and when lowering my hands to my side, the seas calmed as well.

When my hands reached my sides, I lifted my head, meeting Devlin's eyes. My eyes never left him, as I sauntered over to retrieve my mantel from Emily. I made sure to put a little extra sway to my hips. Emily helped me with the mantel, and the three of us headed toward Devlin.

He urged his horse to a walk, meeting us halfway. "Good afternoon, ladies." He inclined his head, his eyes never leaving mine. "Lady Jami, I was just on my way to the keep. I had promised to take ye to see yer sister this afternoon."

"I appreciate it, Lord Devlin, but I no longer feel the need to see her just yet. Emily has promised to give me my first riding lesson and, with the weather so nice this afternoon, I hate to pass it up. I'm sure Blair will still be there tomorrow." I hooked my arm through Emily's. "Shall we head to the stables?"

"Of course, Jami. We need to get ye into a riding outfit before we start though." Emily inclined her head to Devlin. "We shall see ye at evening meal, Devlin." We all walked toward the keep, Drea coming up to take my other arm.

Emily whispered, "Sway yer hips a bit more. He will watch us walk all the way." She giggled.

Drea and I both laughed as well, putting on the front we were just friends out enjoying one of the last nice days of the season. When we got to the keep, we went in the kitchen door and sprinted up the stairs to my room. We busted in, laughing, and I noticed a pile of clothing on my bed. I stopped and stared.

"Oh good, they got most of them done." Emily floated over to the bed. Rifling through the gowns and day dresses, she pulled out a riding habit that could've come from my closet at home. If I'd owned one, that is. Emily presented it to me. "Here, my dear, is yer riding outfit."

I went over to take the pants and short jacket. A linen shirt went underneath the jacket. "But, Emily, I've never seen you wear pants, not even on horseback."

"That's true, but ye do. Drea told me the first time she saw ye, ye had on an odd pair of pants and I thought, if we want to shake Devlin up, then ye need to incorporate a bit of yer time with ours. Go ahead, try it on. I am already wearing an appropriate dress to ride in, as is Drea."

I took the garments and went behind the screen to change. I came out with the pants on, as well as the camisole slash corset Emily had given me. "I need help with the laces."

"This is a design of my own," Emily said. I heard the pride in her voice as she laced me up. "It shouldn't be as confining as a regular corset, but still give ye enough support to show off yer assets."

When she had the laces tied, she helped me with the cream under shirt. After it was tucked in, I put the short jacket on. The outfit was warm, being made of a heavy woolen material and lined with some type of fur. Emily asked Drea, "Can ye help put her hair up so it will stay out of her eyes, but still draw attention to her face?"

"Of course, a simple plait will work, with a few strands left loose around her face." Drea sat me down facing away from her and started on my hair. Emily located the riding boots she had the servants deliver. I realized we shared the same shoe size. She must have lent me a pair of her own. "There, finished. I can teach ye how to plait yer own hair one evening if you would like. It makes it so much easier when ye are working or outside."

"I would like that." I gave her a big hug. Leaning down, I pulled on the riding boots.

"That's it. Our mounts should be ready by now. Let's go for that ride." Emily grinned.

I giggled, starting to get excited. I'd ridden when I was young. It was something Mother said all refined ladies should know how to do. It'd been years though, since I'd been astride a horse. Emily and I talked about it earlier, and she assured me she had the perfect mount.

We walked out to the stables, and saw three horses ready for us. Emily walked me up to the middle mare and introduced me. "This is Sadie. She is a loving girl and minds well. I think ye two will get along."

I rubbed Sadie's muzzle, then stroked her neck. She shook out her main, and nipped at my shoulder in greeting. I walked around her, inspecting her bridle. The saddle they'd placed on her had straps that were tight and fit well. I rounded her flank to see the most beautiful chestnut stallion I'd ever seen. He was tethered to the gate. I walked over, murmuring comforting words. He shook his head, and I started to hum as I reached him. He calmed immediately and allowed me to stroke his neck and nuzzle up to him.

"You are gorgeous, aren't you? You need to get out and run, don't you?"

He nickered in agreement.

"Shall I take you out instead of good ole Sadie? I think we both need to blow off some steam."

He pawed the ground, anticipating the run we'd have.

Before Emily could say anything, I swung up onto his back and grabbed the reins. I leaned forward to unclip the halter lead from his bit. I moved him as Emily gasped.

"What are ye doing, Jami?!"

"I'm taking this beauty for a ride." I beamed at her.

"Jami, ye can't. That's Christan's mount. He's a war horse," she sputtered.

"Emily, I took years of riding. Just because I haven't been on a horse for a while doesn't mean I've forgotten all I was taught." I saw Christan coming out of the keep. "You girls catch up with me, won't you? I'll stay inside the tree line, but we both need to blow off some steam and just run."

I headed the stallion toward the gates and nudged him forward. He took off at a light canter. As Christan yelled at me, I leaned over the stallion's neck, loosened the reins, and let him set the pace. We shot out of the gate like lightning. I raised my face just a bit to let the wind whip around me, laughing at the feeling of being free. I let the stallion set the course to start with. This was his land and he knew it better than I. After running through a couple of fields, I sat up a bit and slowed him, taking my time to bring him to a stop. I glanced back to see if Emily and Drea were anywhere to be seen. I laughed at how far away they were, and nudged my mount into a walk toward them. I could tell he still needed to run by the bunching of his muscles beneath my thighs. I patted his neck, and leaned down to whisper in his ear, "I know boy, that wasn't near enough. Be patient and we will run again soon. You are like the wind."

I met up with the girls and giggled at their faces. "I swore we would find ye along the path, sprawled and in need of help, but I was wrong," Emily harrumphed.

"I told you I could handle him."

In response, the stallion side stepped a bit, getting impatient to run again.

"He's full of energy and just needs a good run or two to calm him down." I patted his neck.

We walked alongside the girls for a bit. As I chatted with them, my mount started to get antsy, and side stepped again. I tried to calm him, but it didn't seem to help. Then I realized there were hoof beats coming up behind us. I figured out why he was prancing. One of his buddies was coming up beside us, with Devlin astride. I couldn't help but smile at the frown on his face.

"What do you think ye are doing? That mount is not meant for leisurely strolls. He's—"

"A war horse, yes, I know. He needed a good run, so I decided that's what we would do. We are simply walking with the girls for a bit before taking off again."

"He was not meant to be a ladies mount, Jami. He's trained to respond to his master, not to carry silly women around on meandering walks through the heather fields. I'll take ye and get ye properly mounted for this type of riding." It was then that his eyes traveled down the length of me. "And what the hell are ye wearing?"

"It's called a riding habit. You see, when I was growing up and taking lessons, girls wore a riding habit with pants, a jacket, and appropriate riding boots. As far as me being able to handle this mount, I bet I could beat you to the end of the field, around the far tree, and back to the gates."

Devlin actually broke out laughing. "Ye beat me, that's funny. Now enough with the jokes, I am sure Christan would like his mount so he can continue with his patrol." Devlin went to grab for the reins, but I leaned over the horse's neck and gave him a slight nudge, giving him his head. We took off in a shot.

"That's a boy. Let's show Devlin what we can do."

Devlin yelled after me, and his mount attempted to catch up. We were coming upon the tree line and I shifted my weight slightly, gauging how sensitive he was. The stallion immediately banked around the tree. I sat up as we raced, passing Devlin as he tried again to grab for the reins. We flew through the fields, heading straight for the gate. I sat up, feeling free, as if I were flying. I attempted to start slowing my mount, but I couldn't. I knew he needed a bit more running, so I tightened my knees and released the reins, throwing my arms out to the wind, letting it play over my arms and through my hair. The plait Drea had put in was gone now, and the strands whipped around my head. I laughed into the wind, happier than I'd been in a long time. We came up to the gate a bit faster than I wanted.

Christan stood there with his arms crossed. Not a very happy camper.

I took the reins and pulled the stallion up short right in front of him. The stallion, of course, wasn't happy about this and reared so, as I'd been taught, I leaned into him and held on with my legs. I waited until he calmed a bit more before releasing my hold.

I noticed all the guards at the gate had come to attention and were surrounding me in a half circle. Christan closed in on me, ready to catch me if I fell. "Don't worry, dear Christan, I won't fall. I learned how to keep my seat at an early age."

A groom quickly came to take the reins at Christan's command.

Devlin came up behind me as I swung my leg over and reached down to Christan for help in dismounting.

As my feet touched the ground, I met his eyes and saw him smiling. "I didn't mean to steal your mount. He just needed a good run as much as I did." I winked at him.

He leaned down and whispered in my ear, "Just ask me next time. I don't mind, but I am pretty sure Devlin does."

I tucked my hair behind my ear as he leaned away and winked at me.

"I know." I stood on my tip toes and kissed his cheek. "The fire has been run out of him now, so he should be happy to just patrol around. Will I see you at evening meal?" I asked, knowing Devlin was watching the whole interaction between Christan and I.

"If my lady wishes." Christan bowed to me.

"Wonderful, save a seat for me." I strolled through the gates toward the keep.

"And just where do ye think ye are going?" Devlin bellowed at me.

I slowly turned and gazed up at him. "If you must know, I'm going to my room to get ready for evening meal." I walked away.

Devlin dismounted and, throwing the reins to a waiting groom, quickly caught up to me.

"Have ye gone completely mad? That horse could have killed ye," Devlin said as he took my arm and continued to stride toward the keep.

"But he didn't, Devlin. I'm not as fragile as you think I am."

"What the hell do ye think you are doing walking around in men's clothing? Letting everyone see what should be covered by a skirt. Kissing my guards in front of everyone. Do ye want people to think ye are a loose woman?"

I stopped in my tracks. "Is that what you think? Do you think I'd just spread my legs for anyone?" My voice rose as I stood there with hands on my hips.

He faced me. "No, that's not what I think." He ran his hand over his face, blowing a breath out as he did. "I just don't want the other men to think it. The way ye treated Christan just now."

"You're jealous. You aren't worried about what the others will think. It's the fact I paid attention to Christan that's bothering you. If you noticed, no one else standing around paid attention to what Christan and I were doing, they all had their own jobs to attend to." I stepped closer to him, placing the palms of my hands on his chest, trying to control the beat of my own heart. "If you're that worried about it, stake your claim now, in front of everyone, Devlin." I breathed. "Kiss me."

I saw the struggle in his eyes, but his need for me won out. He wrapped his arms around me, encasing me in pure strength and power. His lips made their descent upon mine fast and furious. This was no slow, romantic kiss. This was a kiss to brand, to lay claim, a kiss of possession for all to see. My hands found their way behind his neck, twining in his hair. My body pressed closer, melting into him, and I got as close as I could. He nipped and coaxed my lips open with his teeth and tongue. All thought left my mind. I could only focus on the heat building in my blood, starting in my core and bursting to all parts of my body. I was on fire. My knees went weak, and I would've fallen if Devlin hadn't been holding me.

His hand ran through my hair, and pulled my head to expose my neck. He kissed and nibbled his way down to my collarbone. I couldn't help the little moan that escaped my lips. He growled in response, a shudder going through his body. His other hand stroked my back, moving down to cup my cheek and push me into the evidence of his arousal. He made it quite clear he was just as excited as I was. He returned to kissing my lips, and my conscience decided to wake up. Realizing we were still in the middle of the courtyard, I pulled away before we went too far.

Gulping in air, I searched Devlin's eyes, and saw a pool of passion swirling around. "I need to get inside, Devlin. We're being watched."

He glared at the few men who'd stopped to stare at us. He leaned down and picked me up, startling me. "I can walk on my own."

"Humph," he grunted.

I couldn't help myself. I laughed. I laughed the whole way to the keep.

Devlin set me on my feet, a smile on his face. "Ye enjoy laughing at me, don't ye?"

I ran up the stairs to my room.

CHAPTER 24

Devlin watched Jami run up the stairs, appreciating the way those pants hugged the curves of her body, curves that shouldn't be on display for all to see. His body yearned to follow her, but he restrained himself. He already deemed himself a fool, having kissed her in the middle of the courtyard where everyone could see them. As much as he'd like to brand her for all to see, he still had her virtue to think about. He really didn't mean it when he'd said she was seen as a loose woman, but his jealousy had taken over before his mind could censor what came out of his mouth. Seeing her talking and flirting with Christan drove him mad.

He veered, shaking his head, and went to the gates to check in with Christan and get the guards report. He didn't understand his reaction. He and Christan had both liked the same woman before. Hell, they'd shared women before. This time though, when he saw Christan's hands on Jami, he wanted to rip his arms out of their sockets, throw Jami over his shoulder, and lock her in the tower. These feelings were new to him, but his body seemed to know hers. He knew exactly where to touch or kiss to get her to elicit those little moans that drove him crazy. As soon as they were alone and unclothed, he'd know her body like his own.

Just thinking of all the things he wanted to do to and with her got his blood pumping again. It became uncomfortable to walk, and he started to sweat. He took a deep breath as he reached the gates, finding Christan there waiting for him.

"That was quite a show, my friend." Christan slapped his shoulder. "She is a spitfire, isn't she?"

"She is no concern of yers," Devlin growled.

Christan put his hands up. "No harm meant, Devlin. She's all yers. I don't think I could handle that one."

Devlin walked outside the gates and Christan followed. "I don't know what's come over me, Christan. Every time she is near, my brain flies out the window and I just want to snatch her up and lock us in a room for a week." He ran his hand through his hair. "What am I to do? I have never experienced this kind of jealousy over a woman, especially with ye," he implored his friend.

"Mayhap yer heart knows more than ye think. This may be a time ye need to follow it and have faith. I think she's good for ye. Hell, I think she's good for the clan, no matter where she came from. Have ye noticed how happy the people have been since she arrived? Watch them the next time ye see her walking among them," Christan advised. "She takes the time to talk to each one of them, no matter how young or old. She really is concerned about them and they listen to her."

"That's what scares me the most. She is getting into the hearts of the clan, but what happens when she leaves? Ye and I both know she's not from here, and if ye believe her, she's not even from this time. What is here to keep her?" Devlin wondered aloud.

"Well, it seems to be, ole friend, ye are. I have a feeling if ye just open up and let yer heart lead the way, she would stay."

"When did ye get all wise?" Devlin laughed.

"I just observe well." Christan grinned. "I have no romantic feelings toward her, Devlin. It's more like she's a little sister and I don't want to see either one of ye hurt, so tread lightly, but ye will have to decide soon."

"Aye, I know the prophecy." Devlin strode toward the keep. "Head out and do yer rounds. Evening meal will be soon upon us and yer presence has been requested."

"Very well, I will see ye then, but think over what I have said, Devlin. Don't string her along. Decide either way, and let her know soon, before she becomes further attached to the people and them to her." Christan walked over to his mount, swung into his seat, and headed to the tree line for the last patrol before putting the evening guard on duty.

Devlin went to wash up before heading to the main house to change for evening meal. After a quick dip in the cold wash barrel, he was on his way. It wasn't long before he encountered the old gypsy man.

"Good evening, my Lord Devlin. Ye are just the man I was searching for."

"Good evening to ye, Alexandrou. How is yer family doing?" Devlin inquired.

"They are well, I wanted to let ye know we will be packing up and moving on tomorrow, but I have a favor to ask of ye and yer family."

"What is that?" Devlin asked, a bit skeptical.

"Well, as ye can tell, my eldest daughter Drea has become close friends with Lady Emily and Lady Jami. I think she will do them both a great service if she were to stay on for the winter season. I would ask that ye allow her to stay behind. She would make a great lady's servant, and would be a great help with the children. We don't have much, but I would gladly leave what we have to pay for her room and board," Alexandrou replied.

"There is no need for that, old man. I can see how important she is to both women. I believe Lady Emily has already asked her to stay on. We would be glad to have her stay for the winter, or as long as she likes. An extra hand is always welcome in our home, and she has shown she is an asset to the keep."

"Oh, thank ye, Lord Devlin. I am most grateful for yer hospitality and will be in yer debt." Alexandrou bowed.

"Think nothing of it, ole man. Ye and yers are always welcome in the house of O'Rourke. Ye proved yer worth to my father. I wish ye and the rest of yer family safe journey." Devlin bowed.

Alexandrou walked toward his camp to help his other children finish packing. As Devlin continued to the keep, he glanced up toward the window in Jami's room. He hoped to catch a glimpse of her, but instead he found the curtains closed tight. Heaving a deep sigh, he climbed the stairs and entered the keep, then headed to his chambers to change for evening meal. Devlin made it down to the great room before many of the others. He sat in his chair and enjoyed a leisurely pint of ale as everyone slowly made their way in for the meal. His warriors came in packs, filling up the lower tables. Fran, Connor, Declan, and Christan all joined him at his table. As usual, his little brother, Darrick, was nowhere to be seen, and probably bedding some wench in town. Drea came in and sat with her family for their last meal together before they left on the morrow. Donovan escorted Emily in to the head table. When his eyes finally traveled to the stairs just outside the entryway, he saw Jami. She was a vision of beauty. His mouth went dry, his heart beat faster, and he heard the rushing of his blood in his ears. He leaned forward to watch her walk in.

She wore a dark maroon gown this evening, but something was different. Her hair was pinned up off her neck, and the gown fit her to perfection, hugging her curves before transitioning to a flowing skirt that flirted with her legs. Still, there was something not quite right. As Devlin's eyes traveled down and up, he realized the neckline was definitely lower than anything he'd seen on her before. Not so low as to be scandalous, but low enough to make him lick his lips in anticipation of tasting her skin there. He couldn't take his eyes from her as she made her way through the tables, and right up to his. She meant to sit with him and his guard.

She strolled to Donovan and Emily, and curtsied before coming to sit down. Christan stood to assist her with her chair, and the rest of his guard stood as she sat. He was the only one who hadn't stood in respect.

Jami greeted each of his guard in turn, giving them a smile and a shy glance from under lashes. Why was she playing coy all of asudden? When her eyes met his, her cheeks blushed pink and she bowed her head. "Good evening, Lord Devlin. I hope the rest of your day went well."

"Aye, everything was quiet today," he croaked out. Clearing his throat, he scanned the table. "We are all here, let's eat."

Jami leaned over to say something to Christan, but Devlin couldn't hear what over the din of everyone else talking and eating. She thanked the servant who brought her trencher of stew and grinned encouragingly at the young man. Devlin's blood started to boil. He gripped his eating utensils so hard they left indentations in the palms of his hand. Jami and Christan bantered back and forth and when she laughed, the green eyed monster roared up within him. It seemed Jami sensed it. She gazed toward him and shared a shy smile, soothing the beast clawing to get out.

They ate the rest of their meal with Jami sliding little glances his way every now and then. She was carrying on a conversation with Christan next to her; every time she touched his arm or laughed at something he said, Devlin saw red.. If it wasn't for his excessive training at self-control, he'd have lifted Christan across the table and thumped him a good one.

When the meal was over, many of the men started moving the tables to the edge of the room, and a few of them set up to play music. Obviously, Emily had an evening of dancing and music planned. Christan helped Jami out of her chair and escorted her up to sit with Emily, so the men could move their table to the wall as well. Devlin positioned his chair to watch the dancing as a passing servant refilled his pint.

Out of the corner of his eye, he could see Donovan stand and speak with Jami. Next thing he knew, Donovan was escorting Jami out to the makeshift dance floor. Devlin's jaw dropped ... Donovan never danced. The last time was at his wedding, and that was only because it was required. He sat and watched as Donovan taught Jami the basic steps of the dance. Watching her in another man's arms, even his married brother, didn't sit well with Devlin at all.

"If ye stare much harder, ye will burn a hole through her dress," Christan said to his left. "If it bothers ye that much, go out and dance with her yerself."

"It's not that. I can't believe Donovan is on the dance floor. I haven't seen him dance since his wedding."

"I know, and do ye notice the smile on his face? He seems as if he is actually enjoying himself. See, Devlin, I told ye she has affected everyone in this clan, and in a good way." Christan took a long draw off his pint.

The song ended and Donovan escorted Jami to her seat next to Emily, then took his place on Emily's other side. He kissed her cheek and Emily beamed up at him before turning to talk with Jami.

****

"Devlin couldn't take his eyes off ye," Emily said under her breath.

"Well, he has an odd way of showing his interest." I tried to catch my breath. I hadn't danced that much in a long time. I was most definitely out of shape.

"Trust me. What ye are doing is working. It will take a little time, but stick with it. I see him eating out of yer hand by the end of the week," Emily whispered.

"I don't want him eating out of my hand; I just want him to admit he has an interest and act on it," I said. "I can feel Blair, and she's doing all she can to get out of that cell. If she were to escape in any way, I'd be doomed. I have to get him to admit his feelings before then or my chances are over."

"Don't ye worry. That cell is reinforced with double iron bars, and she isn't going anywhere. And I made sure that cook adds a bit of my sleeping draught to her meals to keep her subdued. Not enough to knock her out, but enough to keep her groggy and off her game," Emily admitted.

"Emily! I never would've imagined you to be so devious." I laughed. I was still giggling when Christan approached the dais.

He bowed. "Lady Jami, may I have this dance?"

I stood and curtsied slightly. "I'd love to dance with you." I took his arm and followed him to the floor.

"Ye are exceptionally lovely tonight," he complimented me. "It's driving Devlin quite mad watching ye."

"Well, if he is so bothered by it, why doesn't he ask me to dance himself?" I retorted.

"Devlin sees ye as a weakness, and he doesn't handle weakness well. Actually, I can't ever remember him having any weaknesses. Give him some time, let him work it out, and until then make him a bit jealous." Christan twirled me around and drew me close.

I laughed. "I think we're off to a good start for that. If looks could kill, you'd be done for." I leaned into him as the music slowed.

As Christan danced me around the floor, I noticed Bran making his way toward us. He tapped Christan on the shoulder and we came to a stop.

"May I tread a measure with ye?" Bran asked

"That's up to Lady Jami," Christan said, keeping one hand lightly on my lower back.

"It's fine, Christan. I'd be honored to share this dance with Sir Bran." I curtsied.

"It's just Bran, ma'am," he replied.

"Very well, Bran."

He took me into his arms, leaving an appropriate amount of space between our bodies. He was light on his feet as he slowly twirled me around the room.

"You're a very good dancer," I complimented him.

"Thank ye, Lady Jami, and ye are as well." The song ended and he bowed. "It was a pleasure dancing with ye."

I curtsied and went to my seat.

Connor came into my path on the way to the dais. "Lady Jami, I hope ye aren't too winded. I would love to ask for the next dance."

"Why, I'd love to Connor." I laid my hand along his arm as he led me to the dance floor. That was how the rest of the evening went, dancing with the elite guard, and even Donovan again.

The evening got later and I was again in Christan's arms. My feet ached and I was tired. I leaned into him and laid my head on his shoulder.

"Are ye getting tired, Jami? I can take ye to yer seat."

"No, let's finish this dance. I'm tired, but I'm having so much fun. Let me just relax a bit here." I closed my eyes as we swayed to the sad song the fiddler played. "This song seems so sad. What is it?"

"It's about a young man who goes off to battle, leaving the woman he loves, only to come home and find his village has been raided and she's dead. This is his song to her, telling her of his love."

"That's so heartbreaking." I yawned.

We heard someone clear their throat behind us. We both stopped to see Devlin standing there. "Christan, I think Lady Jami has had enough dancing for one night." He glared at Christan. "I can take over from here."

Christan bowed to me. "Jami, it was a pleasure, and I hope we can dance together again soon."

I curtsied and almost fell over from exhaustion. "Me too, Christan. I had a pleasant evening." I turned to Devlin and tried to glare at him. "That was rather rude, don't you think?"

"Ye can barely stand, Jami. Don't ye think it's time to turn in?" he asked with eyes holding concern, and controlled hunger, and something else I couldn't make out.

"I'm fine. If you're so concerned, why don't you dance with me?" I stepped up to him and wrapped my arms around his neck. "You seem to be the only man here tonight who hasn't asked me to dance. Come on, Devlin, dance with me," I pleaded. I took a deep breath, drawing his eyes to my cleavage.

He sighed. "All right, if ye agree that after this dance ye will take yerself up to bed. Ye are exhausted, and we can't have ye getting ill." He stepped closer, wrapping his arms around my waist, and leaving no room between us.

"As you wish." I laid against him, my head just barely reaching his chin. I listened to his heart beat as we swayed around the floor. I closed my eyes and let my body feel, every nerve highly sensitive. He drew circles along my spine as we danced. I felt him breathe in the scent of my hair as he tried to pull me even closer, his hold getting stronger. The heat was instant this time, no slow build up. My whole body shot with electricity. The song ended and Devlin's eyes were pools of deep amber. I saw the passion raging, and the evidence of his arousal was pressing against my belly.

"I think it's time for ye to head to yer chambers, Jami. I don't know how much longer I can keep myself under control," Devlin croaked.

I stood on tip toes, and whispered against his lips, "Then don't."

CHAPTER 25

He stepped away and took my hand, wrapping it around his arm. "We must say goodnight before leaving." He half walked, half dragged me to say goodnight to Donovan and Emily. Emily simply gave me a wink with a twinkle in her eye. I didn't care, my limbs were turning to pudding, and if I didn't get out of there soon with Devlin, I'd most likely collapse. Holding onto his arm, I curtsied to Donovan and wished him a goodnight. Then I gave Emily a quick hug and was quickly guided out by Devlin.

He rushed me up the stairs and to my chamber door. I opened it, then pulled him inside with me.

I let go of his arm, closed the door, and replaced the latch. I faced Devlin and saw the struggle he was having. It was written plain as day on his face.

"Jami, we shouldn't do this. It's not right or proper for me to be in here with ye alone."

"I don't care about right and proper. I want you, and I know you want me too. Let's stop fighting this." I walked toward him, swaying my hips, my eyes half hooded, attempting my best seduction. His hands clenched and unclenched repeatedly as he watched me approach. My heart pounded. I was sure it'd jump out of my chest before I reached him. My hands were clammy and I held my breath, waiting for his response.

This was it.

He'd either give in or reject me for good. I was taking a huge chance, stepping out of my comfort zone like this. I'd laid it all on the line.

He raised one hand to my face. Starting at my brow, his fingers trailed across my cheekbone and down my jaw line. When his thumb traced my lips, I opened them and sucked his thumb inside. I grinned at his sharp intake of breath and chuckled, sending vibrations up his thumb.

He pounced. His hands seemed to be everywhere as his lips descended upon mine. My breath left me, and electricity flowed through my veins. With one hand twisting in my hair and his other arm wrapped around me, he lifted me off my feet, his lips never leaving mine, and carried me to the bed laying me softly on the furs.

His lips then left mine to trail kisses of fire down my neck. I leaned my head to the side, giving him more access, and making the neckline of my dress shift lower. Every kiss was a shot of pure pleasure straight to my core, and building in a warm pool between my thighs.

Devlin nipped along my collar bone, licking each one to soothe the sting. His hands roamed over my every curve, making the skin under my dress hyper aware and sensitive. His fingers found the laces at the sides of my dress and quickly untied them. With shaking hands, he peeled my dress down my arms, kissing every inch of skin as he exposed it.

I couldn't take much more of this. I could explode right there. I lifted my hips to help him pull my dress all the way off. He stood to gaze down at me, lying in just my corset and a sheer camisole. Heat crept up my neck under his gaze. I licked my lips and let my gaze travel down his body, at some point he'd divested himself of his jerkin.

Devlin was a glorious specimen of a man.

My breasts ached to be touched, my nipples already straining against the sheer fabric of the camisole and corset. Even that small amount of clothing seemed to chafe my skin.

Devlin slowly rolled me over to undo the laces. Once free from the corset, I could breathe deeper. He flipped me onto my back and dipped his head to take a nipple in his mouth through the sheer fabric of my camisole.

I lifted off the bed at the contact, and sparks of pleasure shot straight to my womb. I couldn't take this slow and steady pace any more. I reached for him, pulling his mouth to mine, and our tongues began warring with each other, fighting for dominance.

He gathered the material of my camisole in his hands, and urged my hips up, bunching it up around my waist. I sat up and raised my arms so he could fully remove it. The cool air hit my overheated skin, and I wouldn't have been surprised if there was steam rising off my body. My nipples puckered at the change of temperature, but not for long.

Devlin returned to nuzzle, and sucked one pert nipple into his mouth, while his large hand plumped and kneaded the other one.

My eyes closed and I rose off the bed again. A moan escaped my mouth, and Devlin growled in response, the feeling of it vibrating through my body. He took his time, lapping and suckling both breasts until I squirmed underneath him. He trailed kisses down my stomach, then sat on his knees and stroked his fingers over my thighs and around my knees. So light it was almost a tickle, but slowly increasing the pressure until my thighs fell open, revealing myself and the evidence of my arousal to him. My eyes traveled down my body to his, my pulse racing, and my breath heavy.

I saw that his straining member had shifted his kilt. I sat up, reaching for the waist, but he grabbed my hands and pushed me to the bed.

"Not yet. If ye touch me now, I won't last." He let his hands trail down my body again, over my breasts where he pinched and pulled my nipples, before continuing on to the curls at the apex of my thighs. I grasped the furs on the bed underneath me, straining to keep my hands away from him. He leaned over to kiss my belly button, then moved lower. I writhed in anticipation, holding my breath, my body throbbing with sensations. With his fingers, he pulled my nether lips aside and blew a warm breath on my most sensitive spot.

I saw stars explode behind my eyelids.

I almost flew off the bed. Devlin rested his hand on my stomach to keep me anchored, and then used his tongue to draw out my throbbing nub, circling it, then sucking it into his mouth. He built up a rhythm that had me moving with him, gasping his name as all thought left my head. He continued his rhythm, stopping every now and then to dip into my passage, tasting and teasing me. Something was building inside me and straining for release. I was on the edge, just a little more, and I'd go over into oblivion. He grasped my thighs to spread me wider, then inserted a finger into my passage.

I exploded, straining off the bed and screaming, "Devlin!"

He stood and shed his clothing.

I stared at him in his full glory, my body still pulsing, saliva pooling in my mouth. "Jami lass, you are radiant," Devlin said in awe. My arms opened to him as he leaned over me, settling between my thighs. I wrapped my legs around him, still throbbing from my last peak, and spurred him on. In one swift motion, he entered me, stretching me to the point of pain, but it was a welcome pain. He slowly pulled out and pushed in, rocking until he was fully seated. I was stretched and fuller than I'd ever been before. He was so deep that he was touching my womb.

He rested his forehead against mine, "Ye feel so good. I don't want to be rough, but I don't know if I can hold myself in check much longer." He kissed my nose, then my lips, the whiskers on his chin rasping against my cheek.

"I already told you, Devlin, I won't break. I can handle it, all of it, and honestly, right now slow and sweet is not what I want or need." He searched my eyes, then grabbed my leg and rolled so I was on top. From this angle, I was able to slip further down him. I gasped at the sensation. I was stretched to the max, and every throb was exquisite pleasure and pain. I placed my hands on his chest. He grabbed my hips and started moving me as he thrust. Our rhythm was a fast-paced, wild ride. I was assaulted with sensations. I let my head fall forward, and mewing sounds came from my throat. Devlin growled low in his throat again. He leaned forward and his lips found my breasts. He wrapped an arm around me, and angled my hips so that I took him deeper yet again. I watched him with wide eyes. The sensations were unbelievable, but that moment, locking my eyes with his, I knew one thing for certain: my heart was his.

Devlin started to rock us, in this position. Each thrust also had him brushing against my already over-sensitized nub. I was so close, flying higher than even before. My walls contracted around him, milking his shaft for all it was worth. Devlin roared at the same time I let out a groan.

We exploded together.

I lost feeling in all my muscles for a few seconds, and Devlin went rigid with the explosion. I felt like I was floating among the stars. Waiting for feeling to return, I smiled.

He slowly relaxed onto the furs and I followed him, languidly curling up on his chest, my face up toward his, reaching for a kiss, with his smile of satisfaction beneath my lips. I could barely keep my eyes open, so happily content and warm from our coupling. Devlin rolled me over and pulled me up against him. He reached over and pulled another fur over us both, whispering in my ear, "Sleep now, my *mo chroi.*"

I laced my fingers through his, and let myself fall asleep.

CHAPTER 26

As I started to stir the next morning, I felt a bit sore, but happier than I could ever remember being. I rolled over to find Devlin fast asleep. The poor man, I had woken him for another round, and he'd woken me yet again last night. We couldn't seem to get enough of each other.

I leaned over and kissed his cheek. He reached out to gather me to his side. Then he opened his eyes smiled down at me, and took my hand, pulling it under the covers to reveal to me how easily his body was ready for mine. That one touch was all it took to get me humming and slick for him. I took him in my hand and stroked his length, watching the way his face changed, the emotions rolling across his brow, and his eyes darkening with passion. I loved having that kind of effect on him, being able to bring him pleasure.

My blood heated and my heart swelled at the knowledge of the control I had over him right now. I scooted down under the furs. Taking him in my mouth, I heard his quick hissed breath. I swirled my tongue around the mushroom-shaped head, sucking and licking the drops leaking out, and enjoyed the taste of him in my mouth. With every twitch of his member, my core got wetter. When he could take no more, he flipped the furs off the bed and rolled me over, sliding down to repay the pleasure. Our lovemaking was slow that morning, and when we came together, staring into each other's eyes, I swear the earth moved.

Devlin paused.

We both sensed it. A click, the final piece of my soul locking into place. I saw the last of Devlin's resolve melting and the love shining through his eyes.

He leaned down, touching my forehead with his. "*Mo chroi*, did ye feel that? It's true." He stared into my eyes with awe and wonder.

"I can't deny it any more. My father told me years ago of a prophecy. I didn't believe him, but here ye are my *leannan*." He kissed me as he pushed us both over the cliff.

Stars burst behind my eyes and memories came rushing down on me. Previous lives with this man by my side, and I knew, deep down, there'd be many more to come.

We snuggled up together afterward, his hand rubbing circles on my belly. "Ye know what this means now, don't ye?" he asked me.

"No, what? Food in bed sounds good to me." I teased "Food and an explanation of those words you called me"

He chuckled. "A grand plan, but no, that is not what I meant. This very minute, ye could be carrying my bairn." He grinned. "It means I will have to make an honest woman of ye. As for the words; those are special *mo chroi* is Gaelic for my heart and *leannan* means lover."

"An honest woman of me; you have no problem with that?" I asked, holding my breath. I couldn't believe my ears. Was he really saying what I thought he was? He did call me his heart and his lover but it was so fast, how could one night make that much difference? Or was it the guilt creeping up, his way of saving my virtue.

"Yes, we will be married before the winter is up," he declared.

I threw my arms up and glared at him. "So that's it, you declare it and it will be so." I threw the covers back and stomped to the wardrobe, oblivious to my state of dress. I turned around with hands on hips. "You think that spending one night in bed with you means that I'll marry you? Buddy, it takes more than that. When I marry, it will be for love, respect, companionship. Not because some oaf declared it."

Devlin lay in bed smiling while I went on my tirade. "If ye are finished now, lass."

I snorted and turned to get a dressing gown. Hearing the furs rustle, I knew Devlin was getting up, but I didn't hear him move up behind me. Then he wrapped his arms around my waist from behind, and rested his chin on my shoulder. "I did nae mean to upset ye. I can't deny I didn't want to believe in the prophecy, even after ye showed up with yer odd sayings, unrecognizable accent, and indecent clothing. I have seen how ye have grown to love this place. Ye truly care for the people and the land. I nae longer deny the attraction and feeling of connection."

Devlin turned me to face him, framing my face with his hands. "Lass, I have never felt like this. Last night, it was as if the world shifted and there's a bond here now that I won't break. If it's soft words and romance ye want, I can try. For ye Jami, I would try. For now, just know that I do love ye, and want to marry ye. The sooner the better."

I laughed through the tears streaming down my face. "Now was that so hard? Much better than just declaring we will get married." I stood on tip toes to kiss him.

"Is that a yes, lassie?"

"Yes, you silly oaf, Yes!" I nodded.

He picked me up and spun me around with joy.

Suddenly, a wailing sound echoed through the keep. My hands itched and tingled. I rubbed them together, trying to get rid of the sensation. It was like they'd fallen asleep and circulation was just returning. That sensation enveloped my body the same way, as though I had pins and needles all over my skin.

A knock sounded at the door.

Devlin retrieved his tartan and donned it as he crossed the room. He opened the door a crack. I couldn't hear what was whispered, but he glanced over his shoulder at me. When he was assured I had the dressing gown tied tight, he opened the door and let Christan enter.

"Say that again, Christan," Devlin instructed.

"A few minutes ago I was checking the guard on Blair, and she fell to her knees, screaming. A dark light seemed to seep from her pores and drift into the ceiling. She collapsed after that, and we haven't been able to wake her since. I came to find ye straight away, Devlin. After finding yer chambers empty, I took the chance you might be with Lady Jami."

I stared at my hands. They tingled as if full of power. I peeked at Devlin, raising my eyebrows.

He nodded. "Try something."

I knew fire was an element Blair had control and use over. I raised my palm toward the fireplace and willed the fire to start.

The fireplace erupted with flame, and then settled to a comfortable blaze. I still had a tingling sensation, more power waiting to be released. I strode to the windows, pulling the curtains aside, and throwing the shutters open. The sky was covered in grey and black clouds. Devlin came up behind me. "She used her powers for evil, Devlin, I won't do that."

He wound his arms around me as I regarded the sky, lifting my hands and releasing the power within me. Lightning streaked through the clouds as they opened up and let rain fall upon the earth. When I sensed the last of the excess power leave me, I dropped my hands and sagged against Devlin.

"That was beautiful, Jami. Ye bring life to our lands." We watched as the lightning continued to dance through the skies.

"Christan, come see this." I reached out for him. He came over to stand with us at the window. I grasped his hand tight. He glanced with concern at Devlin and, seeing it didn't bother him, relaxed and watched the storm with us.

When the rain started coming in the window, Devlin replaced the shutters and curtains, while Christan helped me sit by the fire. I looked at them both. "It's over now. She can do us no more harm. Christan, take a healer down to her and see what they can to do help her. She no longer has her powers and without them, she'll eventually die. We don't know when, but I want her taken care of until then."

Christan glanced at Devlin, who nodded his head, so he left to carry out my wishes.

Devlin came over and pulled me up, sat down in my chair, then pulled me into his lap. "Ye are safe now. We are safe, and it's time to move on. Time to start planning that wedding," he said with a mischievous grin. "We have already had the honeymoon."

I laughed and leaned in to kiss him, just as another knock sounded, this one more insistent than Christan's was earlier. I heard Emily's voice. "Devlin, open up quick!"

I ran to the door to find a bedraggled Emily standing before me. "Emily what's wrong?" I asked as I brought her into the room.

She saw Devlin, and the small smile on her face quickly fell away. "Devlin, its Iona. She's been kidnapped, and yer twit of a little brother has rushed off on his own to find her."

"Iona? Isn't that your sister? I thought she was living with your aunt?"

Devlin sighed. "She is supposed to be, but I got word right before the Festival that she intended to come no matter what Donovan said. I told Darrick because he and Iona were close, and I had hoped he could talk her out of coming. I figured he had succeeded when she didn't show." He gathered the rest of his clothing. "I haven't had time to send word to my aunt to verify she had stayed, since you showed up and my whole world has been realigned." He winked at me as he slipped his boots on.

"Emily, go find Christan and tell him to gather the men and meet me at the gate." She nodded and headed out the door.

Devlin gazed down at me. "I hate to leave ye so soon, my love." He gathered me in his arms. "We were just getting to really know each other." He kissed me.

"You need to go find your brother and sister. I'll be here when you return. This will give me time to plan the wedding with Emily and Drea. I'll be fine."

He nodded. "I know, but, well, just be here when I return. I will leave Christan behind to watch over ye." He kissed my forehead.

"But he's one of your best men. Won't you need him with you?"

"It's because he is the best of my men that I am entrusting him to watch over ye and Emily." He kissed me one last time, then headed out the door and down the stairs.

I ran to my window, pulled the curtains aside, and opened the shutters.

Devlin walked with purpose toward the group of men waiting at the gate. He took Christan aside, and they both gazed up at my window. Christan nodded and headed toward the keep. Devlin raised his fist over his heart as I waved and nodded. Devlin and his men mounted up and headed out the gates at full speed. I raised my head to the skies, asking the elements to stay calm and keep them safe.

"Hurry home to me," I whispered at his disappearing figure.

REVIEWS

If you enjoyed *Destiny Finds Her*, please consider leaving a rating and review on the site where you bought it. Reviews and feedback are important to an author, as well as other potential readers, and would be very much appreciated. Thank you.

ABOUT THE AUTHOR

Mother to two boys, 3 four-legged babies, and wife to a loving husband who doesn't mind the extra voices in her head Miranda grew up on a dairy farm in Illinois, but calls Portland, TN home now. She is an avid reader, coffee addict, and loves her day job working at the local public library. Though her true passion is in creating her own worlds, characters, and stories for her readers.

Website: www.mirandalynn.com
Facebook: www.facebook.com/MirandaLynn
Twitter: @MirandaLynnBks
Email: mirandalynnbooks@gmail.com

Made in the USA
San Bernardino, CA
18 September 2015